Winter Harvester

Book One in
the *Other Magic* Series

Nik DeKasha

ISBN 978-0-578-68038-5

Cover art and design by Alison Mitchell

Printed in the United States of America

Titles in
the Other Magic series:

Winter Harvester
Winter Sight

For Angie, the sister I would have followed anywhere if only I'd had the right powers.

Prologue

In a stone-walled cell that sweated in the dank heat of deep earth, a woman lay curled up in a loose ball. She didn't feel the heat, but even if she had, she would have paid it no mind. She had no spare thoughts, for every moment of every hour was spent pondering the answer to one question: how to send a message.

She rolled from one side to the other. Her long hair, normally deep blond with sunny highlights, lay soiled and knotted beneath her. Her dress tangled around her legs, filthy with dirt from the floor of her cell. Her legs were tan and shapely, her feet bare and grimy. She wasn't sleeping. She wasn't crying.

She was thinking.

While she thought, a figure leaned against a far wall outside her cell, his form concealed in shadows the flickering torchlight didn't penetrate, and watched her.

One

Winnie's damp bangs stuck to her forehead in an unattractive wad, and no matter how many times she swiped them this way or that, they eventually made their way back to the space just between her eyes. She stopped walking and screwed up her brow, forcing her eyes into the unnatural position of trying to focus on the spot directly above and between them. Frustrated, she puffed out a heavy sigh and resumed her brisk walk, determined not to feel the trickle of sweat that the offending hair clump had now produced on the bridge of her nose. With each step, the trickle moved farther down her nose. She could picture it as she walked, one clear, salty streak making its way to the tip of her nose, where it would hang, maddeningly, until its own weight overwhelmed it, and it landed in a dark circle on the front of her blouse.

Damn this summer heat!

As she threaded through the crowds of people on the city streets, she determined to think of something other than her damp, limp hair and her sweaty, flushed face. And when she looked at the people she passed, why shouldn't she forget about those things? It wasn't as if anyone at all was noticing the sweat and damp on her body; they were likely too absorbed by their own streaked faces and drenched clothing. Here on her left, a group of teenaged girls stood with their tee shirts rolled up and tucked into their bras, exposing pale skin that hadn't seen the sun in months. One had unbuttoned her denim shorts in the—probably vain—hope that even that inch of exposure would lead to a drop in body temperature. The girl with whom she spoke, whose deep black skin shone with a film of sweat, had slipped her feet almost all the way out of her flip-flops so that she had to bounce on the balls of her feet to keep her heels from touching the scalding pavement. Both girls fanned themselves with half a newspaper circular they'd clearly split for the purpose. And all of them looked surly.

Surly was the order of the day, apparently. Half a block past the girls, Winnie watched a man hurl himself from the back of a yellow cab, slamming the door before leaning down to yell into its open window, "Come back and get me when you've got a working air conditioner, why don't you?" The man's suit jacket was over one arm, and his tie had been yanked loose. His cheeks were so pink they might have been mistaken for frost-chapped if they weren't also wet with perspiration.

Everyone was hot and sweaty and angry. Dogs that had only last week frolicked ahead of their masters in freshly fallen snow now had to be dragged along on their constitutionals. Babies in strollers, fractious from prickly heat, wailed for relief to scurrying parents sucking down bottles of water. And pigeons, who in years past would have pecked for leavings in the shelter of ash and elm trees, jostled one another noisily for space in the shadows of awnings and street signs.

When she turned the corner, another unexpected sight met her eyes: Macomber Park, which she had passed hundreds of times on the six-block walk from her apartment to her father's rock shop, was a patch of caked mud. For years, she'd noted the changing of the seasons in the warm, green life of that park. In the spring, she'd thrilled at the soft buds that speckled the tree branches with lumps, a joyful pox that infected the maples, a garish pink growth that afflicted the park's redbuds. And at their feet, the deceptive little crocuses bursting through the still-brown grass tricked her year after year into doubting that such delicate little blooms could withstand the chilly night air so early in the season. None of their compatriots could boast such a hearty constitution: look at the tulip with its thick stem! Such a powerful looking flower simply couldn't compete with the springtime endurance of the petit crocus.

In years past, when summer finally took hold after the long spring ramp-up, Winnie once again noted its stamp on the life of the park. The early blooming trees—pretty pink dogwoods and thick, purple crabapples—celebrated the warm breezes of early summer. How delicious their bright, brief colors seemed to Winnie! And how wonderful the promise those warm breezes carried: by the time the petals had fallen from their blooms, the park would be alive with children. The air would buzz with cicada song, and the screams of laughing boys and girls tearing from one side of the park's playground to the other would drive out the memory of winter's and spring's hollow, empty days, when the only sounds to be heard on the street were the impersonal noises of city living: car horns, ambulance sirens, the hum of people and goods simply moving and being moved.

In the fall, when the long, hot days of summer, so desirable in June and so oppressive by August, finally gave way to earlier sunsets and brisk, late-evening breezes, Winnie would linger at the park gate on her way home from her father's shop to watch the changing personality of the playground once again. Children wild after hours in school, some still in their uniforms, tore from one end to the other with the same spirit they'd had only months before when summer had been wonderful and new, but now they were called in earlier, mothers and fathers gathering them up for dinner and homework, pulling discarded sweaters from backpacks as the shadows grew long. The dogwoods that had bloomed so prettily in the spring had long since shed their petals; now, their berries nestled brightly among their deep red leaves. Oakleaf hydrangea took center stage now, many of them still proclaiming healthy, white blooms for weeks after their neighboring trees began to color and drop their leaves. Those lovely pyramid blooms were a reminder, Winnie thought, of the season that was ending but that would return again. They were a promise of sorts: in a few weeks, we'll be gone, they said. But our fire-red leaves will hold on to the last sparks of warmth from hot summer, even when the first snow covers us.

And then the snow. Winnie loved every season, of course, but winter was *her* season, and the blankets of snow and the lone cries of Northern Cardinals were for her as lovely as the verdant colors of the growing seasons. After all, it was no coincidence it was called a "blanket" of snow: no growth could happen without the long rest of winter, when the plants lay dormant in preparation for the hard work of breaking through the cold crust of earth come spring.

Winnie stopped to stare now at the barren ground in Macomber Park. That lovely blanket of snow she'd thought of with so much affection each time she'd passed the park in the winter had liquefied almost overnight with the sudden onslaught of heat. As in many parts of the city, the park's storm drains had been unable to keep up with the sudden rush of melting snowfall, and they'd clogged, leaving standing water in a dirty, sooty pool surrounding them. Every low spot in the park had filled with water, and the ground, still frozen from the deep cold of January—which had become the deep cold of February and then March— resisted its penetration, so that the top layer of ground soil, thawing slowly in the blazing sun, became an inch- deep mud pit. The grass that ought to have been greening up as it came to life floated in brown clumps in the deepest puddles. In stark contrast, those spots high enough to have avoided flooding cooked in the blazing sun. There the grass was just as brown, its still- dormant blades pressed flat against dry, cracked dirt.

Winnie frowned, a wrinkle, hidden by the still- sopping clump of hair hanging between her eyes, creased her forehead. This couldn't continue. Something had to be done! She tossed her head with determination, spun on one heel, and continued the sweaty march to her father's shop.

A cheery bell tinkled as she pushed open the front door of Pete's Rocks and Minerals, and as the door swung shut behind her, Winnie listened to the bell's echo. Although the sign on the front door had been turned to OPEN, the shop was empty, as it nearly always was when Winnie showed up in the middle of the day. Or in the evening. Or on weekends. The shop received very few customers.

The echo of the bell told Winnie all she needed to know about where to find her father, so she didn't bother to call out to him. Rather, she navigated around the dozen or so display cabinets that sat haphazardly between the shop's front windows and its back wall. Winnie had suggested occasionally that Pete should consider organizing his displays more logically...or at all. As it was, thousands of chunks of rock sat helter-skelter throughout the shop: in display cases that had been collected strictly to provide more display space and not for any aesthetic purpose, on floor-to-ceiling shelving that lined the three available walls (and part of the fourth: Pete's burgeoning collection had forced him to push shelving units against the front window glass, a choice that did little to encourage more business since it made it look as though the shop was being renovated or had perhaps been condemned), even in an old bureau that her father had repurposed for housing fragile samples that needed to be seated in padded drawers for protection.

She twisted and turned as she moved through the shop, tripping once over a large, black boulder she was sure hadn't been there the week before, and ducked through the doorway at the back and into the office. Well, the *first* office. Here she sighed, finding exactly what she'd suspected she'd find: boxes. Dozens and dozens of boxes with postmarks from all over the world. Some were properly packaged distribution center boxes, the kind with crisp corners and preprinted address labels, but many, many more of them were home-packed wrap jobs, their crumpled labels hand-printed, their fillers—repurposed, yellowed newspaper and half-popped bubble wrap that had probably cushioned the travels of a great many items before coming here, their final resting place—disgorged and piled, forgotten, beside their torn carcasses. Winnie made a halfhearted attempt to pick up bits of torn-off packing tape and several sheets of mashed tissue paper, but upon discovering the trash can already overflowing, she gave up and dropped them back onto the floor.

All of these packing materials had met their end. She silently endeavored to come by Saturday to break down the boxes and deposit them in the recycling Dumpster in the alley, and she'd roll up all the plastic packing materials and haul them to the supermarket to stuff into their plastic bag recycling depository. There was no sense in organizing the material for reuse: her father's shop was a terminal, not a transfer station. Many, many packages came in, but none ever went out.

Kicking aside packing peanuts—and cursing their sender; did they have any idea how hard it was to dispose of those things properly?—she peered down into the open trapdoor that led to the second office, the *real* office. The steps leading down were shadowy, yet

8

a faint light revealed itself the longer she gazed down them and her eyes adjusted to the dark. Already her hair was drying, and just the thought of the cool, dank air at the bottom of those steps began to erase the memory of the intense sunshine outside. She sighed again.

"Dad?" she called into the dimness. "Are you down there?"

His answer was faint but immediate: "Winnie? Is that you? I'm down here!"

She stepped with care down the stone steps, trying to avoid scraping her heels on the rough risers. She wore flip-flops most of the year to keep cool, but normally she opted for sneakers on the days she came into the rock shop. Sandals weren't safe footwear for the floors in her father's office, but the oppressive heat outside had made her desperate, and the thought of spending the day in sweaty, damp sneakers had made her cringe that morning as she dressed.

At the bottom of the stairs, the light from her father's office was brighter, but the air was chilly and still. Goosebumps rose on her arms, and the hairs at the nape of her neck brushed damply against skin that had been sweaty and prickly only a quarter of an hour ago. She yanked the cord to illuminate the overheard bulb mounted at the mouth of the rough-hewn tunnel that led to the office and picked up the flashlight she kept tucked in a niche at the bottom of the stairs. Her father had no problem seeing in the dark; he could easily navigate the stairs and the tunnel before reaching the light switch in his office, but Winnie wasn't blessed with his preternaturally good night vision. She swept the light from side to side as she made her way toward the dim light, scanning the floor for hazards.

Unexpectedly, a shadow cut off the light ahead. Winnie paused and looked up to see the outline of a giant man filling the timber-reinforced doorway. His shoulders spanned the space so that to pass through, he'd have to turn sideways. Though his outline was shadowed in the back light, it was clear that he was stooping; to walk into the tunnel, he would certainly have had to hunch down to avoid cracking his head on the ceiling.

And what a head! The man's pate was utterly hairless, as round and smooth as a riverbed pebble, but a pebble of unprecedented size. It sat like a giant, polished finial on his broad shoulders without the apparently unnecessary detail of a neck to support it.

One of the man's giant hands rested on the unfinished jamb, while the other hung at his side. Even in outline, Winnie could make out the shape of a large crack hammer, one intimidating point casting its shadow on the floor between them.

Winnie grinned. "Hi, Dad." She raised the flashlight just enough to illuminate the giant man's face without blinding him altogether. Pete Harvester's grin, visible now in the light from Winnie's flashlight, was identical to his oldest daughter's. He turned to move out of the doorway so that she could enter, and she rose onto her tiptoes as she passed to kiss his dusty cheek.

"Hello, daughter. I didn't think you were coming by today. I'd have stayed aboveground so that you didn't have to come all the way down here."

"That's okay, Dad. I only decided this morning to come by. Anyway, you know I don't mind coming down here. So nice and cool..." Winnie pulled the chains on a couple more exposed bulbs hanging from the ceiling and switched off her flashlight, laying it on one of her father's several workbenches. "What are you working on down here?" She sneezed twice in quick succession. "Seems dusty, whatever it is."

Pete's eyes lit up. "Take a look at this!" he exclaimed, setting down his hammer and moving his daughter aside by grabbing her by the upper arms, picking her up off the floor, and setting her down again two feet to the left. He turned to the workbench she'd been standing at and began gathering up bits of chipped rock he'd apparently been pulverizing before she'd shown up.

"Dad, you could have just said 'move it'." She poked a pointed toe between his feet to hook the flip-flop that had fallen off when he'd lifted her. Another reason to wear decent footwear down here.

He turned to look at her, confusion knitting his brow. Even then, no wrinkles creased his smooth, round head. "What do you mean?"

"I mean you didn't have to...never mind. What do you want to show me? Some new rocks?" Winnie craned her neck to see what he held. There was no point trying to explain. Her father was *in his rocks*, as her mom called it, and that meant his focus was powerful and immoveable.

He turned to hold up the flaky bits in his hands. "Not a rock, Winnie. A mineral. Talc! I just got it this morning from a contact in China. Have you ever seen this shade of green in a talc sample? I've seen this green elsewhere, of course…olivine is really what I'm thinking of…but this deep and clear of a color in talc is really phenomenal. Have you ever seen anything like it?"

When he turned to look at her, his eyes glittered the very shade he was describing.

Winnie smiled. "No, I can honestly say I've never seen talc that color, Dad."

He smiled back, popped a handful of the talc chips into his mouth, and began chewing. "They taste as good as they look." When he'd swallowed, he put a hand on her shoulder and smiled down into her face. "Now, what brings you by, Winnie?"

His teeth were as green as his eyes.

Two

Winnie reemerged into the noticeably warmer air of the upper office a few beats ahead of her father. She stepped back to give him space to lift and lay down the heavy oak door that covered the entrance to the inner office, and then she unrolled the braided rug that covered it. It was a mostly ceremonial process: it was rare that anyone but a Harvester saw the inside of the storefront much less the inside of this office. But her father had spent years covering this opening, years going back far before Winnie was even born, and old habits die hard. And although she and Pete rarely discussed it, Winnie knew that the inner office was only the first of dozens, perhaps hundreds of deeper, darker antechambers that only he navigated. Likely, only he would be able to navigate into and around most of them. The cold in the inner office bothered Pete as little as it bothered Winnie, but some of the tunnels leading away from that chamber emanated warm air, and Winnie could only imagine how deep and hot some of his hidden spaces must be. Unlike his daughter, Pete was as impervious to heat as he was to cold.

Once the trapdoor was safely concealed, Pete turned an appraising eye on his daughter.

"I know you didn't come by today to listen to me talk about talc," he said. "So why the surprise visit? Something on your mind?"

Winnie crossed her arms and looked around the office, pushing aside a wad of crumpled newsprint with the side of her foot. "Well, I think the first thing we need to discuss is the state of this room. How many deliveries does this mess represent, Dad?"

Pete looked around the room, apparently doing some mental calculations. "Well, I didn't keep count...," he trailed off, his meaty hand stroking the rough skin of his cheek.

Winnie rolled her eyes, but she couldn't help grinning. "Dad, I'm kidding. I don't care how many deliveries you get. But this room! It's hazardous. What would happen if a fire broke out in this room while you're underground?"

Pete chuckled, moving a pile of empty boxes off of a folding chair and settling himself down. The chair voiced its opposition with an ominous creak that Pete didn't seem to notice.

"Winnie, fire can't hurt my specimens. Do you know how hot it would have to burn to melt rock? The chance of a fire burning that hot here...well, it's just not possible. I mean long before that could happen, someone would call the fire brigade, and they'd be in here so fast..."

Winnie didn't need to respond. She crossed her arms, watching as her father contemplated his own words, imagining like she was the aftermath of firefighting efforts in the shop: firefighters digging through the rubble for hotspots, investigators studying the space to understand where the fire started and how it spread, the burned remnants of the rug no longer concealing the door in the floor. How long before it was pried open? And how long after that before crews were in his inner office? Exploring his tunnels? Exposing the depth of his underground expeditions?

And what then?

"Maybe you're right, Winnie. Maybe I need to stay on top of this a little better."

"I agree. I'll be here Saturday to help you get a handle on it, and then how about if you make it a point to take a load of stuff out to the alley every night. Deal? It doesn't have to be perfect, but that will help it stay manageable."

Pete rose, pulling his daughter into a hug. Winnie pressed her face against her father's chest, hard as granite. "You're a good girl, Winnie. You always think of ways to keep me in line. What would I do without you?"

Fifteen minutes later, having cleared a space at the battered kitchenette table and brewed two cups of coffee in the mini pot her father kept for just such a visit, Winnie sat down to explain what she had really come to the shop to discuss.

"Dad, we have to talk about Verna."

Pete lowered his eyes and set his steaming cup on the table. His straight back curved forward, and his strong shoulders sagged. In seconds, he transformed from the powerful brick of man who'd filled the doorway in the tunnel when she'd first arrived to a defeated husk, and Winnie swallowed with guilt at having brought on the change.

"I'm sorry, Dad. I know you don't like to talk about it. I feel terrible too when I think about it. But have you

15

been outside? It's terrible out there! It's March, but it feels like July! Nothing is growing or blooming properly, and there's so much runoff from the snow that the storm drains are all backed up. People are hot and sticky and short-tempered...and who can blame them? They're confused. They don't know what's happening with the weather. And that's just here in the city. Have you been keeping up with the farm reports? Farmers are scrambling to figure out what to do. When this happened last year, everyone just assumed it was a fluke: one year of hot spring weather and a crippled growing season, but everything would go back to normal. But it's not going back to normal, and now no one knows what to do..."

"And you think I do?" spat Pete, standing so suddenly that Winnie jerked back, sloshing coffee onto the tabletop. "What would you like me to do about it, Winnie? I don't have anything to do with any of that. You know that. Why don't you talk to your sisters about it? Maybe the three of you can figure something out."

He turned his back on her, dumping the coffee remaining in his mug into the utility sink he used to clean samples and then pausing, the weight of his broad shoulders supported by the edge of the sink as he rested his hands there.

Winnie took a few deep breaths, needing the time as much as he did to calm down. Her father had never had a temper: he was a steady, slow-moving man, a man happy to be sedentary and still. It wasn't like him to erupt this way, and she knew that was proof of how deeply the disappearance of her younger sister Verna had affected him. It had affected her too, and her sisters and their mother. They were all feeling the strain, but avoiding discussing it wasn't helping the situation.

"I know you don't know what to do either. You, Mom…none of us knows what to do. But it's clear that doing nothing at all isn't helping. I'm not here because I want you to fix it; I'm here because we've all had months to wonder and think, and it seems to me that now is the time to talk about it again. Maybe something has changed. Maybe one of us heard or saw something that could make a difference. I think it's time we all sit down together and discuss it."

"You're talking about your mother."

"Not just Mom. Autumn might have heard something. She usually has her ear to the ground. Even Meri might have picked up on something without realizing its importance. But yes, I think Mom is the one most likely to have heard something."

Pete sighed and sat down across from his daughter again. He still clutched his mug, and he raised it momentarily as if to take a drink before recollecting he'd dumped out its contents. Winnie almost smiled at the dejected look on his face as he gazed into his empty cup. But she caught herself: it wasn't really the coffee he was missing.

"Winnie, you know how your mother can be. Once she's set a course, she doesn't bend. She's relentless. She's made up her mind about Verna, and no amount of talk from you or me is going to convince her to start searching. Have you seen her lately?" He looked up hopefully.

"No. You know how she gets when the ground is frozen. It's another reason I thought now would be a good time to reopen the subject. Now that everything has thawed, she won't be so cranky. She'll be more open to talking about it, don't you think? And if we could get Meri to work on her...well, Meri always has been her favorite."

"That's not true!" Pete was, of course, obligated to say this as the father of both girls, but while he said it loudly, he clearly lacked conviction.

Winnie grinned. "It's okay, Dad. You don't have to pretend. I know Mom and Meri have a special bond. Anyway, why would I care? Obviously, I'm *your* favorite."

Pete threw back his head with a laugh. "I can neither confirm nor deny that, Winter." His face turned grave again as he studied her. "I love you. You're my oldest, and there's no doubt you're the smartest of you four. But this is a fool's errand, Winnie. Your sisters have carried on without Verna, and your mother has made up her mind about her disappearance. It's time for you to move on. Those people out there, the ones you're worried about? They'll adjust. And if they don't, their children will. In a few generations, they won't know anything was ever different. People learn to live with change, Winnie. Time for you to do the same."

Three

Winnie walked home in despair. The tuft of damp hair once again stuck to her forehead, but she didn't bother to brush it aside. What difference did it make that it was early evening and the temperatures were still hot enough to make her blouse stick uncomfortably to her back? As her father had said, it was time to adjust. She was simply going to be hot, *this* hot, until September.

The walk home from Pete's Rocks and Minerals was a matter of only a few blocks, but by the time Winnie rounded the corner to her building, her feet were dragging as if she had walked for hours. It wasn't just the heat...although that was certainly contributing to her malaise. She simply wasn't built for this weather. But the closer she'd gotten to her home, the more she'd felt the weight of her burdens. She'd left Pete's resolved to adopt his attitude: Verna was gone, and the world would simply have to adjust. But each step seemed to chip away at that resolve. Despite her mother's protestations, Verna's disappearance simply couldn't be chalked up to running away. Why would she do that? Verna wasn't an unhappy woman, and she and her sisters were as close as any notably different but loving siblings could be. The four sisters were involved in one another's lives; they talked weekly if not daily. They shopped together and went for coffee. And if from time to time they squabbled in the way that all siblings did—Verna and Autumn had once stopped speaking for a whole season over an off-hand remark about pumpkin spice that Autumn, in the way only she could, took personal and enduring exception to—they never really separated from one another. Those little squabbles went the way of winter snowflakes and fall leaves: coloring the backdrop of many a scene but fading from thought and memory with the next sunrise. There had been a great many sunrises in the lives of all the sisters, but the sisters themselves had endured, stalwart support for one another year to year, crisis to crisis, partner to interminable partner.

And then one day…gone. Verna was simply gone. No note, no strange behavior in the days leading up to her disappearance. Just an apartment standing empty, the door closed but unlocked.

Winter had assumed the worst from the beginning. Surely something had happened to her sister, something that they needed to take immediate action to remediate. But true to form, her family had had completely different reactions. Autumn, glum and pessimistic as ever, said why bother? Verna was her own person, and if she had chosen this path—or if it had been chosen for her—what could they do to change things? And Brooke, the girls' mother, had been even more resistant to Winnie's pleas to launch a search. Verna was no child, after all, and if she chose to disappear, why should any of them involve themselves? After all, Brooke pointed out, there was no sign that Verna *hadn't* left on her own: her apartment was messy but not unusually so. Verna was always messy. The door had been unlocked, but the lock was intact: no one had pried it or broken the door open. The windows in

Verna's apartment were open, true, but it was mid-June. The weather had been delightful, and all of the girls enjoyed the fresh, warm breezes at that time of year.

And to be frank, Brooke had insisted, wasn't it just like Verna to simply run off? She was a woman who enjoyed new experiences. Perhaps she'd met someone. Perhaps she'd seen a picture of a city she simply had to visit. When there was something new to be had from life, Verna pursued it. Just watch, Brooke had said. She'll be back when the seasons change. She'll be back when whatever new thing she's off chasing ceases to be new. She'll be back.

Her father, solid, distracted Pete, had only shrugged. He had learned long ago that Brooke's will was immoveable: what she didn't get immediately, she got eventually, wearing down people over time, her grudges long and her memories longer. If your mother says to let her be, he had told his firstborn daughter, then let it be. If Verna wanted to return, surely she would in time.

Meri had been Winnie's only ally, watching her sister's animated pleas through the orange ringlets that seemed perpetually to bounce in front of her face. Meri had listened considerately as Winnie explained that Verna would never have left without at least explaining to one of them why or where she planned to go. And she wouldn't have left without her things! Her apartment was still full of her clothing, her makeup, her personal belongings. Where could she have gone without her toothbrush and pajamas? Without the thermal mug she used every single day? It simply didn't make sense. For a while, Winnie thought Meri would agree with her, that she would take her side to petition their parents to mount a search. But Meri was…well, Meri was Meri. Was she really listening attentively? Or was that simply the face she wore when she knew she ought to be listening when in fact she was picking out the call of a perturbed chickadee through the open window? As it turned out, the chickadee had won the battle that day, and Meri had given Winnie a loving hug and a winning smile and trotted off into the city to do whatever it was her flighty little heart told her to do.

So Winnie, dispirited by her family's reaction and at a loss as to what she could do on her own, had let the idea of finding her sister go. Perhaps their mother was right…perhaps Verna would reappear after a few months. Surely she'd be home after the first of the new year…

But the new year had come and gone, and snowy days had turned to summer haze overnight, wreaking havoc on farmers and critters and everyone else. And no Verna.

That had been a year ago, and now the same thing had happened again: Winnie need only look at the still-bare trees casting their feeble shadows in the blazing summer sun to see just how great her sister's absence still loomed. When would her family finally see sense?

These thoughts weighed heavily on Winnie's mind that night as she drank a bottle of wine alone in her apartment and ate dry cereal out of the box for dinner. She slept poorly, waking often and drifting in and out of the same dream in which she sank into muddy puddles up to her knees and couldn't pull herself out, only to wake twisted in the damp sheet that was all the covering she could stand in the hot, moist air of her apartment. She awoke mid-morning feeling more tired than she had when she'd gone to sleep, her teeth hairy and her skin sticky with a film of wine-scented perspiration.

She might have spent the day lounging on her small balcony, reading a book and snacking away her hangover, but she and her sisters had a standing lunch date on Tuesdays, and if morose Autumn and inconsistent Meri always managed to show up, she could hardly be allowed not to. She showered and dressed, wrapping her stout form in a maxi dress. She was too busty for a strapless dress like this, and it got caught up on her round hips and behind, but she had never cared much about those things. Meri had bought her the dress this time last year at one of the little sidewalk sales that boutiques set up when the weather is nice and customers prefer to stay outside instead of wandering in to browse and spend.

"It's perfect for you!" Meri had squealed after Winnie had opened the gift bag. She'd held it up to Winnie's front. "Isn't it darling? I just knew you'd love it."

Winnie had looked down at the dress as Meri held it against her—or at least at the elasticized bodice, which was the only part she could see over her own bosom. She'd lifted one leg straight out in front of herself and saw that her foot was entirely hidden by fabric: the dress was at least five inches too long for her. It would have to be hemmed.

Meri had continued to smile into Winnie's face. "Don't you just love it, Winnie? Isn't it just so you?"

It's so you, *Meri,* Winnie had wanted to say. Meri, with her small chest, broad shoulders, and narrow hips, was made for maxi dresses. Even the color, a deep emerald, was better suited to Meri's orange curls and hazel green eyes than to Winnie's white-blonde shag and cornflower irises.

Looking at her sister's guileless smile, Winnie grinned. "I love it. Thank you, Meri. It's just perfect." How could she say anything else?

Once hemmed, the dress had been ideal for the long season that followed, and standing before the mirror in it again now, Winnie found herself once again thanking her sometimes-capricious sister for the gift. She slipped on black flip-flops and headed for the door, grabbing sunglasses from the entry table before heading down to the street. She wasn't *very* hungover, but the blazing sunlight pouring in through the transom seemed particularly bright. She put on the sunglasses even before she opened the building's front door and stepped out.

If it hadn't been for the lingering hangover from the night before, for the glaring brightness of the summer sun, for the sharp pain in her temple when the sun caught her eye and made her wince and drop her head to shade her face, she probably never would have seen the single crocus growing through the cracks in the sidewalk at the bottom of the steps.

Four

It had taken weeks of planning, but once the idea had taken root, it had niggled at the woman's brain relentlessly. The cell itself was impenetrable: iron bars and stone walls without a crevice to speak of. It occurred to her that the cell must have been made especially for her; how else to explain the lack of cracks or seams, places where dirt could hide? So, she'd made a habit early on of looking beyond the bars for useable materials. There wasn't much she could see outside her cell; the space was lit by standing torchieres, and their flickering light illuminated only small circles, leaving the farthest reaches of the room in deep shadow.

Almost from the beginning of her incarceration, she'd known her silent watcher was lurking in those shadows, and as time went by, she'd developed a sense for when he was and wasn't there. Initially his presence had frightened her, and she'd pleaded for release. After a while, both his silence and the fact that he'd pushed her into a position of having to beg him for anything at all had infuriated her, and she'd screamed at him through the bars, using words that she normally wouldn't think of hurling at another being. But finally, she'd become resigned to him, and after more days and nights than she could have counted, she'd begun chatting with him, asking him questions about who he was and where she was and why he was holding her in this prison. She became inured to his silence, resigned to their one-sided conversations in which she wondered aloud about her sisters and parents. And as time went by, she gradually became accustomed to her new life: she woke up one morning to find a bed had appeared, a simple cot with a down blanket, but an improvement on the abrasive stone floor on which she'd been sleeping. Some days later, she awoke to a small, rough-surfaced escritoire, an addition she puzzled over since she had neither paper nor writing utensils. But those too appeared as time went by, and soon she was locked in a room rather closer to a study than to a prison, with a straw mat beneath her feet and a row of books lined up where the floor met the wall.

She'd been sitting at her little desk, paging by candlelight through the newest volume to have mysteriously appeared in her cell, when she'd sensed movement behind her and turned to see that her watcher had slipped away. By now, her golden hair had grown several inches longer, and the dress she'd worn in the first days after her arrival had long since been replaced by a plain, off-white robe of soft cotton with a belt of the same material. But thanks to two tubs of fresh warm water that appeared each morning and a pretty silver comb that had sat atop the first clean robe, she looked considerably better than she had when she'd first awoken in this dark place.

As she sat gazing at the place where her captor normally lurked hidden in shadow, she suddenly became aware of something she'd never noticed before: a ribbon of loose pebbles and dirt a few feet from the bars. It must have been left there by the feet of her visitor after endless days of walking back and forth from…wherever it was he went when he wasn't here.

Certainly, if it had been there before now, she'd have noticed it.

Her pulse quickened. Back when the tubs of bathwater had first appeared in her cell, the plot for escape had bloomed in her mind. She had in those tubs the first precious ingredient she'd need to leverage her unique talents to save herself, but she needed something else: arable earth. But where to find such a thing in a cell made of stone?

For days, the fragile bud of hope had thrived in her heart, and she spent the time when her watcher was absent crawling along the floor, digging her fingernails into the places where the bars met the floor, where the floor met the walls, anywhere she thought a few bits of earth, no matter how small, might be hiding. But as time went by and the dirt she so desperately needed remained elusive, the tubs stopped being a source of hope and became a mocking reminder of how close salvation could be, if only…Gradually, the hope in her began to fade.

But that little bit of dirt outside her cell walls made it flare to life again. If she could just get to it…

She thought back over the previous few visits from the stranger. How long was he normally gone? How much time did she likely have to execute a plan before he'd plainly see what she was up to?

Finally, she decided it really didn't matter. Nothing ventured, nothing gained. She would have to strike while the iron was hot.

Untying her robe and yanking her arms out of it, she pushed herself against the bars closest to the path of scattered dirt. The iron pressed against her ribcage. Slipping her slender arm through the bars, clutching the robe at the end of one sleeve, she flung its other end as far from herself as possible and onto the dirt. The breeze created by the drifting garment lifted some of the smallest particles, blowing them away from her and clear of the robe's reach. She sucked in her breath and held it, watching anxiously to see if she had inadvertently blown away the particles she was trying to collect. When all was still again, she lowered herself to her knees and slowly drew the robe toward her. When she'd gotten it close enough, she gingerly lifted the robe and looked underneath. She hadn't gathered much, but beneath the fabric were speckles of brown. With the gentlest touch, she brushed the little bits of dirt off the robe and onto the stone floor just outside the bars. At this rate, it would take ages to make a pile, but what difference did that make?

If there was one thing she seemed to have plenty of, it was time.

Five

Winnie froze. She stared hard at the fragile bloom open like a pale purple teacup in the hot, mid-morning sun. A man walking a dog tromped past it, and a moment later, from the other direction, a woman pushing a stroller, followed closely by a small child on a training bicycle, passed it as well. Miraculously, none of the passersby, two-legged, four-legged, or wheeled, crushed the bloom. Winnie blinked, daring her vision to clear. Without taking her eyes off the flower, she reached up and gingerly removed her sunglasses, headache and hangover forgotten.

She moved slowly down the concrete steps, not looking to either side. She'd used these stairs thousands of times, and her feet carried her without hesitation to the gate that separated her building's path from the world beyond. The gate's metal was hot under her palm as she pushed it open. She crept closer to the flower. A breeze picked up, and the delicate stem of the tiny plant bent toward her. Its petals were a pretty lavender at the tips, but they faded to pure white at their base. And in the center, a throat of deep yellow, so rich and warm that it was nearly orange, stared up at Winnie. She felt as she looked down into its vibrant depths that it wasn't a flower at all, but an eye, gazing up at her as if to say *I see you, you know, just like you see me.*

Winnie swallowed. She crouched down to study the fragile bloom, setting her satchel down beside her on the pavement. If more people passed as she hunched there, transfixed, she didn't notice them. She reached out one tentative finger to stroke a petal, afraid that she might discover it wasn't a real flower at all but only her imagination. But when her fingertip met the silky surface of the bloom, she knew without a doubt that it was real. There was a real snow crocus, a Blue Pearl, blooming in a sidewalk crack where no crocus had bloomed before. No bulb could have been planted there, and even if one had been, the dearth of crocuses in Macomber Park proved that it wouldn't have bloomed. There was only one explanation for its sudden, miraculous arrival.

Verna had sent it.

Winnie dug around desperately in her satchel, searching for her phone. She had to get a picture. She had to tell her sisters, but telling them wouldn't be enough. She wanted proof. Under her breath, she cursed the shadowy interior of the shoulder bag. Fashion be damned! The bag was like a black hole when it came to heavy items dropped into its depths. She'd complained a dozen times about how hard it was to find anything— keys, phone, pocket umbrella—once she'd deposited them inside. And a continuing fear that the flower might disappear if she looked away, that some magic in her gaze was keeping it upright, meant she couldn't look for the phone as she dug. With a grunt of frustration, she tipped the contents of the bag out onto the sidewalk and groped through them until she finally found the cool, sleek rectangle of her smartphone. She swiped at the camera icon without needing to look at it and centered the flower in the shot. She tapped the shutter icon repeatedly, moving the phone microscopically to the left and right, up and down, to get the best shot. When she was satisfied she had what she wanted, she finally sat back on the sidewalk, letting out a breath she hadn't realized she'd been holding.

She scrolled through the pictures from the first to the last, and it wasn't until the last came into focus that she noticed something else about the shot. There were feet in it.

Squinting, she tipped her head back to look up at the person to whom the feet in her shot were attached.

"Hi!" said a voice. It was a woman's voice, but that was all Winnie could make out about the form that loomed over her. Looking up into the sun as she was, the figure was only a dark shape framed by a corona of bright light. "Do you need help? Did you drop your purse?"

The figure stooped just then to begin scooping up the contents of Winnie's purse. Winnie recoiled at suddenly finding herself looking directly into the space where the newcomer's head had just been and which was now a direct sightline to the blazing sun.

"Gah! Damn, that's bright," she wheezed, squeezing her eyes shut and feeling around for her sunglasses.

"Oh, gosh. I'm sorry!" The newcomer straightened again to throw Winnie back into shadow, and Winnie collected her dress around herself to clamber to her feet. With her sunglasses on and their heads more or less level, she was finally able to make out the face that belonged with the feet. She knew this woman. Didn't she? She certainly looked familiar.

"I live in this building," the woman said as if reading Winnie's thoughts. "In fact, we're neighbors. Well, up-down neighbors." When Winnie didn't respond, she continued, "I mean to say that you live above me, and I live above you. Oh, no. Scratch that. You live above me, and I live *below* you. Clearly we both don't live above the other. That makes no sense."

Winnie, finding this last statement to be the most sensible thing to have happened in the last five minutes, smiled brightly.

"Of course," she said as if she actually remembered this neighbor. "I remember. Your name is…um…"

"Nina," she said. "Nina from 1B."

"Hi, Nina."

"Hi, Winnie," Nina said, and Winnie felt a little ashamed that this woman knew not only which apartment she lived in but also her first name, and she, Winnie, wouldn't even have given her a second glance if they'd passed on the street. "Do you want to put this stuff back in your purse?"

Winnie realized Nina was holding most of the contents of her purse. Hastily, she dropped her phone into it and held it open for Nina to deposit her belongings in.

"Thanks, Nina. I was just in a bit of a rush to find my phone to snap a picture of that crocus."

"Oh, how pretty!" Nina exclaimed, peering down at the little bloom. The wind shifted, and it seemed as though the flower turned to point its saffron-colored eye at Nina. "I didn't notice it when I left for work this morning."

"No, I didn't notice it when I came in last night, either." They stood gazing down at the flower together, and Winnie was suddenly lost as to what to say. She wanted terribly to get going to meet with her sisters and share the pictures she'd just taken, but it seemed rude to excuse herself. Nina had been so nice to stop and help her, and she certainly didn't seem in a hurry to rush off. Winnie was in plenty of time to make it to lunch anyway; there was no reason not to be polite.

"So, you're coming home from work now? Are you on a lunch break?" Winnie asked. Nina could have been at work only a few hours if she'd left just that morning.

"Oh, no. I got fired."

Winnie looked at the woman standing beside her. She was just exactly Winnie's height, but she had a slimmer build than Winnie did. She wore thick glasses with red plastic frames that should have clashed with the scattering of orange freckles that decorated her nose and cheeks but instead seemed to match them perfectly. Her brown hair was pulled up in a lopsided ponytail, and wisps that had come free clung damply to her cheeks. She had thick bangs, long and unevenly cut, that she swept repeatedly off to one side. Each time she did, she pushed her glasses up her nose. They slipped down again immediately as she stood gazing happily at the little flower.

"I'm sorry to hear that," Winnie managed, but it was a half-hearted apology. From the look on Nina's face, it didn't seem like *she* was particularly sorry.

Nina finally noticed Winnie's gaze. "Oh, gosh! You don't have to be sorry. I'm not. It wasn't the right job for me."

"Do you mean that it didn't make you happy?" Winnie asked charitably.

"No, I mean that I was terrible at it. My boss was really nice, and I think she felt bad saying how terrible I was, but I already knew it, so maybe it was less bad for her. I hope so. She was really nice." Winnie felt this didn't bear repeating since neither she nor Nina was likely to have anything to do with this mystery wonder-woman in the future.

An image popped into Winnie's mind, and she snapped her fingers. "I remember! The mobile dog-wash. You drive the van that washes people's pets. I remember seeing you getting out of the van last fall." Winnie looked up and down the street as if the garishly-painted vehicle had been hiding in plain sight all along.

"That wasn't me. Oh! I mean yes, that was me, but that wasn't my job."

Winnie cocked an eyebrow.

"Sorry, I mean to say that *was* me, and that *was* my job, but that was two jobs ago. No, three. I forgot about the ice cream truck."

"Ice cream truck? The weather has only just warmed up. You drove an ice cream truck over the winter?"

"Yes. It didn't work out."

Winnie had to exercise extreme self-control in her response. "Well, I suppose these things happen."

"Oh, yes. And to me in particular. I'm cursed when it comes to jobs. I can't find the right one for me, and

I'm terrible at practically everything I try. I don't suppose I'll ever find my niche, but it won't be for lack of trying." Nina said this with such optimism that Winnie couldn't help smiling even though her common sense was forcefully suggesting this conversation was nothing to smile about. Winnie herself had never been fired from a job, but she suspected most people wouldn't be so happy about the situation.

"I'm sorry to have to run, Nina. It's been nice getting to know you, and I really am sorry about the day you've had, but I've got a lunch date I'll be late to if I don't skedaddle."

"I understand. Don't let me keep you. I've got to go in and find a new job anyway."

For the first time, Winnie noticed the folded newspapers under Nina's arm, and she felt an unexpected jolt of regret at running off when this woman, who was surprisingly close to her from one day to the next, could likely use some commiseration. But it took only one glance back at the crocus to remind her that she herself had a crisis brewing. She struck a compromise.

"I really do appreciate you stopping to help me, and I'm sorry to have to cut our conversation short. Why don't you come down to my apartment tonight for a glass of wine? I could help you go through the job listings."

Nina's eyes lit up. "Would you really? That's so nice of you, Winnie!"

The two women finalized their plans, and with a parting wave, Winnie headed up the street to hail a cab.

Even without the unexpected delay, she'd have rushed
to see her sisters. What would they make of the crocus?

Six

"It's a flower." Autumn peered at the image on Winnie's phone without enthusiasm, her grey eyes hidden behind heavy, black-framed glasses. The three women sat in a small corner table, the one Frances, owner and manager of The Buttercup Café, always reserved for them. As it had been when their threesome was a foursome, it was set with four place settings, the empty chair held in perpetuity for the return of the missing Harvester sister. Their food had not yet come, but the girls had nearly drained a bottle of champagne already. Winnie's hangover, which had crept back into her consciousness on her way to the café, evaporated as she worked her way through her second mimosa.

"It's a crocus, Autumn. A *snow* crocus." Winnie looked to Meri for support, but Meri was huffing into a spoon and trying to make it stick to her nose.

"And...?" Autumn made to pass Winnie's phone back to her, but Meri reached for it first.

"Let me see the croquette," she demanded, snatching the phone.

"Croquettes are an appetizer, Mer." Autumn rolled her eyes. "Why would Winnie take a picture of fried food on the sidewalk?"

Meri, whose immunity to Autumn's criticism and sarcasm had become robust over the years, smiled blithely. "Wouldn't you? It's not every day you find perfectly good snacks just lying around on the ground." She studied the picture on the screen as her sisters exchanged glances that said *bless her heart.*

"It's not a croquette, Meri. It's a crocus. They're flowers that bloom right at the end of winter. They're the first flowers of spring, and by summer, they're gone."

"Not all of them," Autumn cut in. "Some bloom later."

"But this one doesn't. That's a Blue Pearl. It's a spring-bloomer. And even if it were the type that bloomed late, why would it be blooming now? It would be way too soon." Winnie turned away from Autumn's skeptical gaze and pulled the phone out of Meri's hand. "Meri, you agree with me, don't you? This isn't a fluke. That's a spring flower growing where it shouldn't, when it shouldn't. You see what it means, don't you?"

Meri pushed a curl out of her eye and looked into her sister's face. Of the four of them, Meri was the most flamboyant, the most carefree. She was the best sister for sympathy and commiseration, the worst for keeping secrets, and the absolute bottom of the list for puzzling out the answer to a riddle. So it came as a shock to Winnie when she finally answered.

"You think it's Verna? You think she's trying to send you a message or something?"

Winnie choked on her mimosa. When she'd regained control of herself, she reached out and grasped her sister's delicate hand. "I do. Yes, I do think that. Do you think it's possible, Mer? Do you think Verna sent that flower to get in touch with us?"

Whatever Meri was about to say in response was interrupted by the arrival of their lunch. When napkins had been unfolded and a second bottle of champagne had been placed in the ice bucket on the tableside stand, Winnie turned to her sister again.

"Well? What do you think?"

Meri had taken a bite of quiche, and she chewed it thoughtfully. Winnie, sated by the mimosas and too anxious to eat anyway, watched her as the seconds ticked by. Meri kept chewing. And chewing. Autumn, who had taken two bites in the time Meri had been working through her first, put down her fork and looked pointedly at her sister.

"Meri, you're eating eggs, not steak. Swallow already and answer." Winnie glanced at Autumn thankfully. Say what she might about Autumn, Winnie could always trust her to be frank.

Meri finally swallowed and said, "I just don't know, Winnie. I mean, why would she contact you and not one of us? Why not Mom or Dad?"

Because I am the most sensible of all of you. Because Dad wouldn't notice a flower if it was growing between his toes, and Mom won't believe a thing unless she sees it with her own two eyes.

She bit back that thought and said instead, "Maybe she thinks I'm the one most likely to act on a hunch. The one most likely to consider the possibility that something bad has happened and that she might need our help."

"It isn't much to go on," Autumn cut in. "What if it's just a flower?"

"What if it isn't?" Winnie could hear the desperation in her voice; she knew her sisters weren't convinced. True, it was a small clue. True, too, that her father had been right when he said that the world at large adjusted to changes: rivers and lakes dried up, land eroded and changed shape, habitats moved. The living things that inhabited them, human and non-human, plant and animal, learned to adjust. But the changes her father had been talking about were big ones that took generations to perform. How could one little bulb whose genes told it when to lie dormant and when to grow change its patterns in only a couple of growing seasons? It just didn't make sense.

"I get that you're skeptical," she said to her sisters. "I admit that this isn't much to go on. But I have a gut feeling about this. I know Mom thinks Verna left of her own accord, but that never sat right with me. I think something happened, and I think Verna needs us to find her. I don't want to make trouble with Mom, and I don't want to make trouble for you two with her either. But I can't worry about that right now. I have to think about Vee." Using the nickname only the sisters used was calculated, and Winnie felt a twinge of guilt at appealing so obviously to their sisterly sympathies, but she could feel the tide of the conversation moving in the wrong direction. Whether her sisters truly believed Verna had run off, or whether they simply found that explanation to be the most comforting, she didn't know. It didn't help that it was their mother's explanation; Brooke was a force to be reckoned with, and her powerful personality invited no dissent. Winnie herself avoided getting on Brooke's wrong side and could hardly blame her sisters for feeling the same way.

Both Autumn and Meri looked down at their food, unspeaking. Winnie looked from one to the other, but she didn't really need to hear what they would say next. The sisters had made their decision, and Winnie knew she would have to take the next steps to find their absent sister on her own.

Seven

After brunch, the three sisters shopped, wandering at a snail's pace into and out of boutiques and booksellers they had frequented for years. They bought ice cream cones and ate them, dripping and messy, at a park. Meri, who never went anywhere without a sketch pad and pencils in her satchel, settled down in the grass to draw. Autumn sat with her legs crossed on a park bench, her mahogany hair pulled into a neat bun at the back of her head and her glasses slipping continually down her sweaty nose. She grumbled about the heat and about the mess the ice cream made. She grumbled about the glare of the sun in her eyes and the itchiness of her sweater sticking to her skin. Meri suggested she take off the long-sleeved top if it was bothering her, but over Autumn's head, she caught Winnie's eye and winked. Autumn was a sweater girl and a grumbler. The suggestion of a solution was just a courtesy.

No more was said about the crocus or about Verna, and although Winnie enjoyed the hours she had with her sisters, she found her thoughts returning often to the pavement in front of her building. She was anxious to get back and begin planning her next steps, but the plan to begin planning seemed easier to think about than the plan itself. When she tried to formulate how she would begin searching for Vee, her mind seemed to go blank. And when that happened, she was thankful for her sisters, thankful to be sitting and listening to Meri prattle on about baseball games and snorkeling and seashells. Thankful even for Autumn's whinging about seasonal allergies and mosquito bites and open-toed shoes (at this last, she visibly shuddered, looking down for reassurance at her own sensible ballet flats). Their comfortable, sometimes mindless chitchat distracted Winnie from her worries, and although she disagreed with their confident assertions that Verna's disappearance was likely temporary and nothing to fret over, she appreciated their casual company. Like the fourth empty chair at brunch, Verna's absence had a presence all its own. She didn't doubt Autumn's and Meri's affection for Verna, and she knew that they, like her, felt the space left by their missing sibling.

It's just that Autumn is too pragmatic to think anything unusual might have happened, and Meri is too sensitive to imagine something bad, she told herself. They were so different, the three of them. It wasn't surprising, really, that neither sister shared Winnie's view.

As the afternoon began to fade, the women headed back toward the café. Meri had left her bicycle chained to the rack there, and Winnie and Autumn said their goodbyes to her before hailing a cab to share. Winnie watched her sister as she pedaled away, her ginger curls streaming out behind her in the breeze. As she passed, two shirtless boys with several inches of boxer short showing above their low-slung jeans looked up from their phones to take in her tan legs and broad, bare shoulders. They said nothing to one another but looked after her for a long time.

Winnie settled into the back seat as the cab pulled away from the curb. She was gazing out the window, trying again to focus on the plan she'd have to design sooner rather than later but that persisted in turning to smoke in her mind, when she felt Autumn's hand on her arm. She turned to meet her sister's russet brown gaze.

"I know you're thinking about Verna. If things were reversed, and you were the one who had disappeared, and she were the one sitting here thinking about what to do, I'd say don't do anything stupid. But the fact that I'd have to say that to Verna is exactly why I don't think you should make a big deal about that flower."

Winnie's brow creased. "Huh?"

Autumn rolled her eyes. "What I mean is that Verna is the type to do this kind of thing. I know you and Mom don't always see eye to eye, but you have to admit that she really could be right about all this. Verna never thinks before she does things; if you were missing, she'd be the first one of us to go chasing after any little suggestion of a clue, no matter how feeble it may be."

Winnie felt herself bristle at Autumn's suggestion that the crocus was a feeble clue.

"You know what I mean, Winnie," Autumn said in an uncharacteristically soothing tone. "I mean that Vee is impetuous. She follows her heart, not her brain. And you don't. So that's why I'm saying that I don't feel like I need to remind you not to do anything stupid. Because I know you wouldn't. Right? You're not planning to do anything I should be worried about?"

Winnie took a deep breath. Autumn could be sharp-tongued, but she was worried about Winnie, and that touched her.

"I'm not planning to do anything stupid," Winnie responded. She felt this was a truer statement than saying *I'm not planning to do anything you should be worried about.* She smiled at Autumn, and Autumn smiled back somewhat skeptically, it seemed to Winnie.

"If you really feel like you have to do something, just consider talking to Mom about it first. Okay?" Winnie nodded her assent, and the two women passed the rest of their cab ride in silence, each lost in her own thoughts.

Winnie had just finished mashing avocados for guacamole when she heard a knock on her door; she called out to Nina that she'd be right there and set the bowl of dip on the counter on her way to the door. She'd busied herself puttering around her apartment after she got home from her afternoon with her sisters, wiping down the counters in the kitchen and folding a load of laundry, but her actions had been automatic. Her mind had been elsewhere, her thoughts scattered and bouncing from the crocus—still valiantly standing, she'd noted when she stepped out of the taxi in front of her building—to Vee, to her sister's advice in the back of the cab.

Autumn's entreaty, though well-intentioned, had complicated Winnie's thoughts rather than clarifying them. The choice before her ought to have been clear: pursue the message she believed Verna was sending or don't. But there was more to it than that. Exploring whether or not the crocus would lead her to Verna seemed a clear choice, but her sisters didn't agree, and who else's counsel could she possibly take? Was she simply seeing what she wanted to see? Wasn't it possible the opposite was true, and they were ignoring what they preferred not to see? If she struck out on her own, would her sisters support her decision?

And if she was worried about her sisters' reactions, what about Brooke's? Her sisters were her strongest allies; they may not agree with her choice, but they would ultimately come to terms with it. They may even decide she was right after all and join her search. But Brooke had drawn her line in the sand after Verna's disappearance. She wouldn't accept the crocus as a sign of anything other than Winnie's overactive imagination, and if Winnie pressed the issue, Brooke was sure to see it as a personal revolt against her. Brooke could be irrational, stubborn, and vindictive. Because of those things, Winnie tried to stay on her good side; in spite of those things, Winnie felt deep affection for her mother and did not want to cause her more grief than the disappearance of one of her children was likely already causing. Brooke revealed little, but Winnie never doubted her mother loved them all and was suffering from the trauma of losing one her daughters.

If she left the issue alone and took her family's counsel to wait out Verna's absence, she'd keep the peace with the people who meant the most to her. But if the crocus really was a message from Verna, and Verna truly needed her help, how could she not help her?

She was dizzy from so many swirling thoughts, so when Nina knocked, Winnie sent up a little word of thanks for the distraction. She was going to have to figure out where her loyalties lay, but she wouldn't have to do it tonight.

"Hi, neighbor!" Nina trilled happily when Winnie opened the door. "I'm not early, am I? I forgot what time you said to come, and I was afraid that if I waited until later, you'd think I was being rude, so I figured better to come a little early and risk catching you still getting ready than come late and risk being, well, late." Nina kept up this chatter as she moved past Winnie's beckoning arm and scooted, half-turned, down the hallway to the kitchen. It occurred to Winnie that she didn't need to direct her to the kitchen: Nina's downstairs apartment probably had the same layout.

"You're right on time," Winnie finally responded when Nina paused to unstrap the messenger bag from across her chest. "Is your wine chilled? I have a bottle of red we could open in the meantime if it needs to go in the fridge for a bit."

"Oh, perfect," Nina gushed. "I'll put it in."

Winnie was accustomed to her sisters moving effortlessly around her apartment, digging through her cupboards and taking her books and clothing without asking, so it didn't strike her immediately how strange it was that Nina, practically a stranger, now stood before her open refrigerator, gazing unselfconsciously at Winnie's condiments and exclaiming over a jar of specialty olives. Was this normal? she wondered. Was it typical that women simply shared these intimacies with other women? The truth, she realized, was that she really didn't know because Autumn, Meri, and Verna were the only friends she'd had for…ever? That couldn't be right. She wracked her brains, thinking back to friendships she'd had in the past, but even though her mind reversed through the years with impressive speed, no faces came to her.

There were certainly male faces along the way, of course. She was nowhere near as sociable as Verna, but she was a good deal more so than Autumn, so it had always seemed to her that the number of men she'd admitted into her heart or bedroom or both was perfectly appropriate. Her love life hardly bore comparison with Meri's since Meri found all genders equally appealing and therefore had a considerably larger pool to draw from. But many of the men in Winnie's life had been friends, hadn't they? She tried to imagine Nina as a man; would she feel this complete lack of distress if Nina were a potential bedmate? She thought not. Familiarity takes time, after all. And yet Nina's presence in her kitchen—now, specifically, in the cupboard above the dishwasher where she was admiring Winnie's glassware and picking two bulbous, stemless wine glasses—seemed perfectly natural.

Winnie realized that Nina was still talking, yet Winnie had no idea what she was talking about, lost as she was in her own thoughts. She listened carefully to the next few sentences to see if her mental presence had been missed.

"…well, the guy was really nice about it and said that he normally charged people if they broke anything in the store, but in my case, he would be happy to waive the charge if I'd just settle for the items I'd already picked and check out. So, I told him that would be fine, and that's how I ended up with three identical flutes and one that's really close but not quite the same. It's not ideal, of course, but if he had charged me for all the ones I broke, then I'd be…well, I'd be broke too!"

Winnie grinned at Nina's obvious delight at her own wordplay. "You'll have to show me some time," she said, pleased that Nina apparently hadn't noticed how much of their conversation had gone in one of Winnie's ears and out the other. "Want to sit at the kitchen table? We can spread your ads out there and go through them." She motioned to the stack of newspapers Nina had deposited on the counter.

The two women carried their full wine glasses to the table. Winnie fetched the guacamole from the counter while Nina spread out the wanted pages on the kitchen table under the light of a modern, three-bulb chandelier. They sat beside one another, each armed with a red pen.

"Here's to finding a job you're really happy at," Winnie proposed, and Nina tapped her glass against Winnie's and took a long draught. Winnie raised her eyebrows in a mixture of surprise and admiration. Clearly, Nina meant business.

"Well, if I do, it'll be a first," she said after swallowing another mouthful of wine. She scooped a mound of guacamole out of the bowl with a tortilla chip and angled it to fit the whole thing into her mouth in one bite. Winnie's regard for her new friend ratcheted up another couple of notches, and she reached for a handful of chips as well.

"You've never had a job you liked?" she asked.

"Well, it's not so much that I haven't liked any of them—although there have certainly been many that I hated. It's that I never seem to make sense in the jobs. I'll get a job I enjoy, like the dog-washing van, but I'll be terrible at it. Or I'll get a job I'm great at, like being a nanny, but I can't stand doing it. It never seems to match up."

"Was it the kids you didn't like?"

"What kids?" Nina looked at Winnie with one eyebrow raised perplexedly.

"The kids you were a nanny to. Were they what made you dislike the job?"

Nina threw back her head with a laugh. "Oh, no, I was never a nanny to actual kids. Human kids, I mean. I was a nanny goat."

Winnie looked at Nina blankly. "You were a what now?"

"A nanny goat. Well, a goat nanny. I worked for a guy who bred those little goats people keep in their homes as pets."

Winnie felt her mouth hanging open and snapped it shut. "People keep little goats indoors?"

"Oh, yeah. They're pretty popular, too. This guy I worked for bred them on the side, so he hired me to stay at the house with them during the day while he went off to his real job. I kept them company, took them for walks, made sure they were fed and watered. I was really good at it, but I just hated it. The breeder was so nice, and I knew he'd be sorry to see me go, but I had to give him notice." Nina looked wistfully down at the newspaper page open before her. "Nanny notice. I felt ba-a-a-a-a-d," she said, drawing out the word in an uncanny impression of her discharged charges.

Nina's face was so serious, and her bleat was so unexpected, that for a moment, Winnie simply stared at the strange woman sitting beside her. And then she did something she hadn't done in a long time: she snorted.

The blast of her sudden mirth was so loud in the small kitchen that Nina startled, and when she turned to look into Winnie's face, something between the women broke loose. Winnie began shaking with laughter so powerful that it was nearly silent, and Nina's whoops were the only sound until Winnie managed to control herself enough to gasp for breath. Nina stood up, clutching her side and guffawing, tears shaking at the corner of her eyes in time with her spastic laughter.

Finally, after much sighing and eye-wiping, both women managed to calm down enough to refill their wine glasses and resume their search, but their focus was tenuous. Winnie hiccupped once and set Nina off on a giggling spell, and minutes later Nina caught Winnie's eye and grinned, and even that small suggestion was enough to make her snicker and forget where she was on the page.

When a real sense of calm seemed to have reasserted itself, the women once again settled into their search, and Winnie felt herself relaxing, the mixture of good wine and exhausting laughter doing more for her sense of ease than she could have hoped. How long had it been, she wondered, since she'd focused on a task? Since she'd lost herself in something positive? Since she'd laughed until her stomach muscles ached? She couldn't think of a single time since Verna had disappeared, and she smiled to herself at the thought that this near-stranger had been the source of renewed happiness.

But hard on that thought came guilt: did she have the right to be laughing and drinking with a girlfriend when Verna was missing, especially now that she was so sure Verna was in some kind of trouble? Wouldn't she feel terrible if their roles were reversed, and she were somewhere in need of help, and her sisters were off living their lives and drinking merlot instead of exhausting themselves searching for her? Her smile melted into a frown.

"What's the matter, Winnie?"

Winnie's head shot up, and she realized Nina had been studying her face while she'd been lost in thought.

"Nothing, really. I have stuff on my mind. But it's nothing related to your job hunt. I'm totally focused on this." She gestured to the spread sheets of newspaper, marked and dotted with red ink.

"Oh, I wasn't asking because I thought you weren't working hard enough. I asked because you looked really sad. Like, *really* sad. Are you okay? Do you want to talk about what's wrong?"

Winnie was surprised that her first impulse was to spill the whole story to Nina, but Nina hadn't come over tonight for tea and sympathy, and Winnie's burdens weren't Nina's.

"No, but thank you, Nina. I really want to help you find the perfect job. Let's focus on that."

Winnie was surprised when Nina stood abruptly and began gathering together the pages they'd been milling over. "You have, Winnie. You've helped me do that."

"You found one you want?" Winnie must have been more lost in thought than she'd realized if Nina had found what she was looking for without Winnie noticing.

"Nope. I didn't find a single thing I think I'll actually enjoy," said Nina as she folded the mass of papers into clumsy fourths and stuffed them into her messenger bag. "But I'll apply for all the ones we circled and hope for the best."

"So I haven't helped you at all, Nina!"

Nina reached into the fridge and then turned to Winnie with a grin, the now-chilled bottle of chardonnay in one hand and a corkscrew in the other.

"You helped me a lot, Winnie. You helped me eliminate all kinds of jobs that I definitely am not interested in, and you helped me relax after a crummy day. So I say we take a break."

"Well, you've convinced me," Winnie said, holding her wineglass up for a refill. Her little sliver of guilt about distracting them from their task melted in the light of Nina's smile. "Let's go in the other room so we can put our feet up. I wonder if I have ice cream?"

Ten minutes later, wine glasses refilled and bowls of ice cream in hand, the women settled themselves in Winnie's comfortable front room. Nina had slipped out of her shoes, and she sat in an overstuffed chair with her legs folded beneath her. Winnie lounged back on the couch, her bare feet propped up on an ottoman. She'd moved a window fan from her bedroom into the living room. The stifling heat of day had given way to a cool—if somewhat humid—evening, and as long as they didn't move around too much, they were quite comfortable.

Winnie had just leaned her head back against the cushion when Nina said, "Okay, go."

Feeling that she was already becoming accustomed to Nina's lightning-fast conversational turns, she simply grinned and said, "Okay. Where am I going again?"

"Tell me what you were talking about at the table, the thing you have on your mind."

Winnie sat up straight. Accustomed as she may be becoming to Nina's quick manner, she clearly wasn't used to her candor. And yet why shouldn't she confide in Nina? She had exhausted the resources available to her: her parents and her sisters. She had no girlfriends to act as sounding boards, and maybe what she needed was the chance to talk through things with someone who was disinterested. Nina would bring fresh eyes to the problem, and she certainly wouldn't be shy about voicing her opinion about what Winnie ought to do.

"Well, I have to be honest with you, Nina. My problem is kind of...unusual."

Nina's eyebrows shot up. "Ooh, let me see if I can guess!" She sat back in a pondering pose. "You're dating a married man, but you've secretly fallen in love with his son? No, that doesn't seem like something you'd do. Oh! You've inherited a fortune, but you're concerned your newfound wealth will ruin you?" She leaned forward, eyes shining, before Winnie had a chance to respond. "You received a message from beyond the grave, and now you have to decide what to do with the information?"

Winnie's mouth dropped open.

Seeing her sudden change of expression, Nina slapped her hand over her mouth. "Oh my gosh, Winnie. I was only joking! Which one of those is right? Please tell me it's the inheritance because I can definitely help you figure that one out…"

"It's the last one, actually," Winnie responded. "Well, I hope it isn't really the last one because I think I have received a message, but I hope desperately that it's not from beyond the grave."

"Go on," Nina urged, sitting back in her chair and cradling her wine glass as if settling in for a long story. "Who do you think you've received a message from?"

"My sister, Verna," Winnie answered. "She disappeared a little over a year ago, and we've never had any idea what happened to her, but I think she might have sent me a message today."

Nina rose and crossed the room, plucking a framed drawing of the four sisters from Winnie's crammed bookshelf. Tucked in the corner of the frame was the original photo that had inspired the drawing.

"Did you draw this?" Nina asked, glancing up from studying the sketch.

Winnie shook her head. "My sister, Meri. She can't sit still. She's always drawing something."

Nina plucked the original photo from the frame, replaced the drawing, and crossed back to sit beside Winnie on the sofa. "This is you with your sisters?"

Winnie nodded, pointing out Verna's smiling face. "That's her there."

In the photo, the girls were gathered at the beach. Winnie stood at one end of the four, a straw hat shading her face. She wore a black one-piece with a tropical print sarong wrapped around her waist and tied over one curvaceous hip. Beside her, Meri stood a head taller, her bright yellow string bikini contrasting beautifully with her deeply tanned skin. Her wild curls, caught in a frozen breeze, formed a corona around her smiling, freckled face. Winnie's arm encircled her slender waist. Beside Winnie's pale but pretty skin, Meri's brown complexion looked burnished.

Meri's arms rested on her sisters' shoulders: Winnie's on one side, and Autumn's on the other. Autumn too wore a wide-brimmed hat, and she wore a long-sleeved, dark purple one-piece. Her hair was pulled back in its perennial bun, and her nose was white with zinc oxide. Like Winnie, her figure was more voluptuous, and it appeared even more so in comparison to the two sisters flanking her. The camera had caught her with her mouth open in speech. Beside her, farthest from Winnie, stood Verna. The tallest of the four sisters, she grinned happily into the camera. She held one hand against her forehead to shield her amber eyes; the other hand clutched Autumn's biceps. Her butter-yellow hair hung in a messy braid over one muscular shoulder and fell to her ribcage. She wore a black halter-top bikini with bottoms that rode low on her slim hips.

Nina returned to her chair, picked up her wine glass, and studied the framed photo.

"She's beautiful. You think something bad happened to her? Like maybe she was kidnapped?"

"I don't know. There wasn't anything about her disappearance to make me think she was hurt or got into a fight. Nothing like that. But I don't think she would have just run off. Does that make sense?"

"Of course it does! She's your sister, right? Who would know her better than you? If your gut is telling you something isn't right, then something isn't right."

"You think so?"

"I sure do." Nina leaned forward, tucking her straight, brown hair behind her ear. "I have a brother, and he's basically my best friend. No one knows me better than he does, and I'm sure he'd say the same thing about me. If I had a bad feeling about him, I'd take it seriously."

Winnie warmed with affection toward Nina, and she hoped it wasn't simply because she was telling Winnie what she most wanted to hear. Nina understood siblings, and she believed in instinct. The question was whether she'd believe the rest of the story.

"There's a little more to it, Nina. And you might think I'm kind of crazy..."

"Oh, my crazy meter is pretty poorly calibrated. I'm not in a position to throw stones. Hit me with the crazy."

"It's just that my sister isn't…What I mean to say is that my sister is sort of…" Winnie hadn't explained her family to anyone in so long that she could scarcely remember having done it at all, much less how she'd done in the past.

"Just spit it out, Winnie. What's the deal with your sister?"

Winnie took a deep breath and looked into Nina's eyes. "My sister," she finally managed, "is spring."

Eight

The days had come and gone (she assumed—it was impossible to tell with no access to sunlight), but she had finally amassed a modest pile of dirt using the robe. On the first day of gathering it, she'd gotten too pleased with herself and too absorbed in her task and had nearly gotten caught. The distant creak of an opening door somewhere off in the gloom told her a meal was on its way, and she'd scurried to wrap the now soiled robe around herself and curl up under her coverlet before the hooded figure that brought meals and removed her soil bucket appeared. If there was a face beneath the hood, she couldn't tell: her caretakers never looked at her or spoke, and their hooded forms varied only in height and girth. There was more than one person helping the silent watcher, she knew, but she had no sense of just how many.

She'd watched the hooded figure as it moved into her cell, cursing herself for cutting it so closely. The figure didn't seem to have noticed the concentration of dirt outside the wall, but if it did…Next time she risked the robe trick, she'd have to conceal the dirt somewhere, although where that might be, she couldn't imagine. For now, she just had to hope the figure left as efficiently as it had come and didn't see her secret stash.

That first close call taught her a lesson about caution and concealment, and for the days after, she had limited herself to only a few swipes with the robe, brushing it off and adopting an innocent pose long before she feared a visitor might arrive. Then, she'd carefully gather that day's few particles and place them between the back cover and the final page of one of her books. Five books soon bookended the others, lying flat and stacked one atop the other rather than sitting upright in order to keep their precious booty secure.

Then, one day, as she opened the top book to deposit her latest prize—having spread as much particulate inside the back covers of the four books beneath it as she thought reasonable—she made the decision: she had enough. With this last little pinch, she could put the next part of her plan into action.

She waited patiently for the perfect opportunity, feigning sleep and straining to hear the sound of her captor's exit. When she was sure she had the most amount of time she was likely to have, her dinner having been delivered no more than a few hours previous and no other attendants expected before the next meal, she slipped off her cot and carefully gathered up the stack of books. She worked rapidly, emptying dirt from inside each cover into her palm. When she had every visible speck gathered together, she sat back for a moment, admiring the collection she had managed to put together and smiling to herself at the thought that before long, this ordeal would be over.

She crouched beside the bars closest to the stone wall in the spot directly opposite the shadowed area where her silent visitor normally stood. She emptied the dirt in a tiny pile on the floor between the first and second bars. It looked much smaller on the floor than it had piled in her hand, but that made little difference. For her purposes, it was enough.

She rose slowly, wary of disturbing the air too much and sending any part of her hard-earned treasure airborne. She carefully moved across the cell to her ewer, tipping its fresh contents into her cup and returning to the dirt pile.

She spread out her long body on the floor, her face less than an inch from the mound, her chin resting on the back of her flattened hand. She dipped one fingertip in the cup and gingerly dropped the water that clung there onto the tiny pile. Then she closed her eyes, parted her lips, and breathed gently across the dirt pile, inhaling deeply but slowly to avoid drawing any of the dirt into her lungs and exhaling even slower to ensure she didn't blow any of it away. When she felt still and centered, she ran her tongue once over her dry lips and whispered, "Grow."

The prickle to which she had been long accustomed ran from the bottoms of her feet to the back of her scalp. Her fingertips tingled, and she felt the tiny hairs on her arms and upper lip stand on end as the command manifested within her and passed into the dirt pile. She smiled when a single grain of sand tumbled from the top of the pile.

Hours later, she awoke to a prickling sensation that was completely different. She was facing the wall and could see nothing else, but the sense that someone was watching her was unmistakable. Slowly, she rolled over to peer through the cell bars.

She woke fully and instantly. Her silent visitor, who for months had never stepped out of the shadows, was standing at the bars, watching her. Unlike the attendants that frequented her cell, he wore no cloak, though his clothes seemed to be made of the same rough cloth. He wore straight-legged trousers and a boxy, V-neck tunic. Long, sinewy arms hung from straight, broad shoulders. His hands were relaxed at his sides, and his feet were bare.

Every inch of exposed skin was perfectly white.

She stood slowly as if he were an exotic bird and any sudden movement would frighten him into flight. A small part of her mind registered the ridiculousness of this action: he had kidnapped her, robbed her of consciousness, and incarcerated her here against her will. He'd given her no answers, no information. He was a villain.

And yet her steps toward him were tentatively curious. She studied his face as she moved closer. He was looking at her, watching her closely as she approached. He wasn't quite handsome: his nose was long and pointed, and his forehead was quite high, giving his already tall frame the impression of having been stretched. His hair was black, a startling, messy explosion that seemed totally out of sync with his almost translucent skin. Unsettlingly, his irises were black.

Breathing deeply to calm herself, she approached the bars. He said nothing as she moved, and his eyes never moved from her face. She stopped when she stood only inches from him, separated only by the iron bars, the dank, charged air, and the expanse of purple creeping thyme that had spread from one end of her cell to the other.

She wiggled her toes in the soft spread of leaves and flowers beneath her feet, relishing the respite from the feel of cold stone. Before her, her captor's jaw clenched.

"What is this, Verna?" he asked. His voice was softer than she'd anticipated, and it rasped as though it hadn't been used recently.

"This?" she asked, looking around as if she had only just noticed they were standing in a tiny, indoor field of wildflowers. "This is creeping thyme. Some people call it mother of thyme. I think it's quite pretty." And indeed it was pretty: the single shoot that had sprouted from the pile of dirt had sent feelers to every corner of her cell. Every inch of floor was covered, and when it had run out of open space, it had crept into the closed spaces as well: between her books, under her cot, up the legs of her writing desk and chair by a couple of inches. On the other side of the bars, it disappeared into the darkness, and Verna wondered if it had made it all the way to the door she heard opening and closing in the distance when the attendants entered.

She looked up into her watcher's face again. She was tall, but she still had to look up to make eye contact with him. And she did, unabashedly, quirking one side of her mouth into a grin.

He hadn't moved a muscle, yet she could feel tension in the air around his body.

"Why did you do this?" he asked again in his cadaverous rasp.

At this, Verna, never one to keep her temper in check in the very best of circumstances, broke over him like a wave.

"You have the nerve to ask *me* why *I've* done something?" She wasn't shouting, but her tone suggested she wasn't far off. "You kidnapped me! You've been keeping me in an underground jail cell for like…" She realized she had no clue how long she'd been captive and sputtered before finally spitting out, "Forever! So if anyone in this room right now should be asking the other one 'why did you do this,' I think it should be me. Don't you?"

He didn't respond, and Verna felt her temper rise even further. "Don't you have anything to say for yourself?" She stared up into his face, waiting for an answer.

"Get rid of it."

"Not going to happen," she snapped almost before he could get the entire command out. "If you're going to keep me here indefinitely, then I get to make it more comfortable to live in."

They continued to face one another. Verna had never backed down from a fight, a characteristic her sisters repeatedly pointed out tended to get her into trouble. But in this case, trouble was what she was already in. What further harm could there be in fighting back?

Just when Verna thought she could hold the gaze of those unfeeling black eyes no longer, he dropped his gaze to the leafy mat on which he stood. Shoulders slumping, he sighed.

"Have it your way," he said. "But no more."

He turned to leave, and Verna was nonplussed to discover she felt let down. Was that it? Had she won the battle with so little fight? She watched his retreating form, his pallid heels standing out starkly against the verdant carpet she had urged into life.

"Wait," she said. He paused but didn't turn around. "Who are you? What's your name?"

She could see his cheekbone in profile as he listened to her. Where his pale skin pulled tight over his temple, she could see blue veins under his skin.

After a few moments of silence, he spoke. "Tod," he said, and then he turned back toward the darkness and disappeared across the amethyst-colored expanse of thyme.

Verna crossed her cell and sat on her cot. She realized as she looked at the place he'd disappeared that she was trembling. She had banked on confrontation, but she had assumed it would be with one of the hooded nursemaids and not with her actual captor. And she certainly hadn't imagined that confrontation ending in her being permitted to keep her creation. She had anticipated being commanded to rip up the creeping blooms, perhaps even being forced to watch as the attendants destroyed them. But this *Tod*, although clearly not interested in explaining her captivity, had decided to permit her to keep what she'd grown.

Not that it mattered much since the creeper had already fulfilled its true purpose. In those first few minutes after she'd breathed life into the dirt and urged it to grow, it had begun its expanse in all directions, and as the first hours of its growth crept by, she had continued to urge it along, pushing it farther in every direction, but particularly across her cell. As she'd nurtured its growth, she'd watched it, closely following the lines of its stems as they spread across the stone, doubling back each time she came to a bloom to find the previous split and follow that line to its end.

The creeper, propelled by her nurturing magic, had grown impossible distances without rooting, so that for hours, as she crawled around the shrinking bare floor on her hands and knees, she saw no new roots, just endless bifurcations leading to new leaves and budding blooms. And then finally, when her knees were bruised purple and her back ached from hunching inches from the floor, it happened. One shoot that had pulled away from the mass and curled along behind her book stack, sending leaves skyward along the way, suddenly sent an offshoot in the other direction, straight down toward the stone floor. Verna had held her breath, hoping against hope that what she was seeing was truly happening.

The tiny shoot prodded the floor like a microscopic finger. It seemed as fragile as a single hair to Verna, and when she realized she was holding her breath, she turned her head slightly to release it, afraid of interrupting the little finger's progress. But she never took her eyes off of it, and as she watched, the miniscule green hair paused against the floor, reoriented itself, and slipped into the stone.

Verna's eyes widened in delight. The little root hadn't really slipped into the stone; it had found the one thing she'd searched for all these weeks—months?—without success: a crack. And where there was a crack, there was something extraordinary. Something that could change the outcome of this nightmare.

Somewhere in the depths of that crack was earth.

Nine

Following Winnie's pronouncement about Verna, Winnie and Nina sat in silence, neither moving. Nina studied Winnie's face thoughtfully, and Winnie waited patiently as Nina's gears turned. She concentrated on breathing slowly and deeply, working to keep her heartrate slow and steady.

Nina took a deep breath and opened her mouth, apparently about to speak, but when Winnie sat forward to hear her new friend's response, Nina snapped her mouth shut with a small *whump* sound. She sat back and took a sip of wine, her gaze moving away from Winnie's face to a point somewhere over her right ear. Winnie resisted the temptation to look over her shoulder to see what Nina was studying, suspecting this might just be Nina's intellectual rumination face.

Something registered on Nina's face, but Winnie couldn't read the expression. Her gaze came back into focus, and she picked up the photo again, studying it with renewed interest.

What if Nina was looking for a nice way to tell Winnie she was clearly unhinged? What if she was trying to figure out the fastest, safest way to escape the apartment? What if she was planning to call the police? Winnie was just about to interrupt the silence to tell Nina she was only kidding when Nina suddenly spoke.

"How do you make it snow?"

Of all the responses Winnie might have anticipated, this one had never occurred to her. Her mouth fell open, and in one irrational moment, her thoughts speedily reviewed her conversations with Nina so far. How many times had Nina said something to which Winnie could conjure no response whatsoever? Either Nina was a remarkable and intuitive conversationalist or Winnie had become dull since the last time she'd had a friend she could confide in. She decided on the former, a more satisfactory interpretation for both of them.

"Umm…," she replied, and in her brain she amended her interpretation somewhat. Maybe both options were a bit true.

"Oh, you don't have to tell me if it's, like, a trade secret or something. I just wondered."

"How did you know I make snow?" Winnie asked in amazement.

Nina grinned and turned the photo toward Winnie, pointing at Verna's smiling face. "This is Verna here, right? Spring? And you mentioned one of your sisters is named Autumn, so I'd guess she's the one here with the long sleeves. She doesn't look like a hot weather girl, so she must be fall." Nina continued to study the picture. "Also, her name is Autumn, which is kind of a clue."

Winnie shrugged, conceding the point.

"So that just leaves this other sister. What's her name again?"

"Meri. Well, she goes by Meri, but it's short for—"

"Summer? That makes sense. She sure looks right at home on a beach. That just leaves you, Winnie. Which I assume is short for Winter?"

Winnie tapped the side of her nose and then looked down at her lap sheepishly. "As far as the snow goes, I just need water. I summon my elemental power and tell it to freeze. And it does."

"Can I see?" Nina gazed at Winnie with a look so guileless that Winnie laughed.

"I thought you'd think I was out of my mind, Nina! You don't seem phased by this at all."

"Well, it kind of makes sense, Winnie. There's been this terrible weather change that no one seems to understand, so something had to have happened. And the flower in the sidewalk today that you were so excited about…That's the message you're talking about, right? You think something has happened to Verna, and she made that flower grow to get your attention so that you can help her, right?"

Excitement surged in Winnie. "Yes, that's exactly what I think! Wherever Verna is, I think she's finally found a way to get word to one of us. I told my sisters today that I think she contacted me because she knows I'm the most likely to recognize it as a message and use it to find her."

"And what did your sisters say? Are they going to help you?" Nina had scooted forward to the edge of her seat. She pushed her glasses up on her nose and brushed her bangs out of her face for the umpteenth time.

Winnie's excitement dissolved as quickly as it had expanded. "No. They're not going to help me. They don't think it's a sign. They think it's just a flower."

Nina's face contorted with puzzlement. "I don't understand," she said. "You guys look so close in this picture, more like girlfriends than sisters. Aren't they worried too? Don't they want to see her come home?"

"Yes, of course," Winnie said, rising to retrieve the wine bottle from the refrigerator and refill their glasses. "It's just that our parents aren't convinced there's anything to be worried about. Well, that isn't really true," she amended. "My mother is convinced she just ran off of her own accord, and my father is convinced it's not worth disagreeing with my mother. My mother is…" Winnie chuckled. "Well, my mother is quite literally a force of nature. So, my sisters aren't keen to move against Mom. And I guess a big part of it all is that it's just easier to believe Verna went off on her own. I hate to think she's in danger, and I'm sure they do too. It's comforting to believe she's just gone off on an adventure."

"And that's something she would do?" Nina asked. "Something she's done in the past?"

"Well, not really. Not like this. But Verna's pretty capricious. If something piques her interest, she tends to follow it without really thinking about the consequences. It's not that she's risky, exactly; she just gets tunnel vision when something interests her. So, it's totally believable that she could have met someone who interested her, and she just followed that person wherever, or she might have heard about an event or a destination that she just *had* to see for herself. It's possible."

"But you don't think it's likely?" Nina pondered.

"I don't. Not for this amount of time. And for her to be gone during her season? Unthinkable."

"Yeah, I don't know your sister at all, but even I think it's weird that she wouldn't be back for something

71

that big." Nina looked down at the photo in her lap again. "So, what are we going to do, Winnie?"

"We?" Winnie gaped at Nina. "Nina, I didn't tell you this because I expect you to help me fix it. This isn't your responsibility. I just needed someone to talk to about it. I felt like no one in my family was really looking at it objectively, and I wanted an outside perspective on it. But that doesn't mean I expect you to help me. Thank you, though! Please don't think I'm not grateful that you were willing to."

Nina unfolded her legs and stood, picking up Winnie's empty ice cream bowl and carrying it and her own to the kitchen. Over her shoulder, she said, "I'm glad we got through that part so fast."

"Which part?" Winnie asked, following Nina into the kitchen to put the bowls in the dishwasher.

"The part where I offer to help and you insist that *no, no, I couldn't possibly ask that.* Now we can both move forward feeling like we've done the right thing." She pulled a notebook and pencil from her messenger bag and seated herself on the kitchen counter facing Winnie. "Now, let's figure out what the logical next step should be to find Verna."

That night, after Nina had returned to her own apartment in the wee hours, Winnie lay in bed exhausted and hungry for sleep yet irritatingly wide awake. She tried to reflect on all that had happened that day: finding the crocus, meeting Nina, fielding Autumn's concerns, revealing her family's secrets, and then...

Planning Vee's rescue.

There was too much to sort through logically; Winnie's emotions tumbled and churned. Against all logic, Nina had simply accepted everything. The story was unbelievable, and yet Nina had reacted like it was all perfectly normal, giving Winnie feelings she hadn't had in months: a sense of control and the hope that she could make the situation better. Winnie was going to find Verna, and she wasn't going to have to do it alone. She'd have Nina by her side.

Initially, she'd continued to demur. She didn't know what the first step should be, she'd told Nina. She didn't have any ideas where her sister might be or how hard she'd be to get to when she did find her. And Nina needed to find a job, not worry about Winnie's family problems.

But Nina had brushed away Winnie's protests with a wave of her hand. For one thing, Winnie's family problems were clearly a little bigger than a typical family's problems. When a normal family had a crisis, it didn't affect weather patterns across the globe. Winnie conceded that point. And, Nina said, unemployment was actually the perfect condition in which to undertake a potentially hazardous and interminable adventure because she wouldn't have to worry about calling in to work or finding people to cover shifts.

"What about your rent?" Winnie had asked, appalled as the words left her mouth that she was asking about something so private. The sudden rush of excitement at the thought that she was finally going to do something to help her sister had gotten the better of her.

But Nina had only grinned. "My brother pays for my apartment. He's single and makes a lot of money, and he's always cared for me."

"That's so kind," Winnie mused, overcome with a sudden tenderness that made her throat tighten up. "He must be such a nice man to do that for you." Winnie welcomed the temporary distraction from her concerns to marvel at the filial love in someone else's family.

"Well, we went through stuff together, he and I." Nina had bowed her head when she'd said this, and Winnie had studied her downturned face. Her glasses had slipped down her nose again, and her bangs obscured her eyes, but Winnie could clearly see that the corners of her mouth were drawn down in a frown. She'd let Nina sit quietly with her thoughts for a few beats and was just about to say something when Nina looked up at her and plastered a bright smile back on her face.

There's something there, Winnie had thought.

"Anyway, the point is that there's nothing stopping me from helping you, and seeing as not having spring is working out not great for people, I think it's some kind of moral imperative or something that I help you."

Winnie took a moment to navigate that sentence and then smiled.

"Even though part of me knows I should tell you I can't possibly ask you to do this for me, Nina, a much, much bigger part of me is so thankful that I don't have to do it alone." And then, more to Winnie's surprise than to Nina's, she'd crossed the kitchen and hugged Nina.

"Aww!" Nina had exclaimed, squeezing Winnie back unselfconsciously. "I'm so happy to help."

And help she had. For the next hour, the women had sat in serious discussion of next steps, planning the best course of action for beginning to track down the source of the crocus. This had mostly involved Nina asking a lot of questions about Winnie's abilities and about the state of Nature, the true Nature that mortals knew nothing about, but fortunately for Winnie, Nina tended to leave very little time for Winnie to respond, so they hadn't gotten too off track too often. Intermittently, Winnie simply promised to explain this and that when they had more time.

While it was true that there was more to Nature—and to the Others who ruled over it—than Winnie could imagine covering in one night, the more complicated reality was that Winnie herself didn't know or understand much about the Others. Nina was likely to have questions Winnie simply would be unable to answer.

"How does Verna grow something?" Nina had asked, getting Winnie back on more solid ground.

"Well, she needs the things most plants need in order to grow: dirt, sun, and water."

"She could be practically anywhere and get those things," Nina observed.

"Yes, I've been thinking that, too. We need a way to narrow it down some. She's clearly somewhere she can't get out of because she wouldn't need to send a message otherwise, and she must not be anywhere that has access to a phone. But she's by water, dirt, and sunlight, so she has to be in pretty good shape. I mean, she's not in a dungeon or anything, right?"

"Hmm…You're sure that's all she needs?"

"Yes?" Winnie had thought she was sure, but as she considered it more, she felt less confident. Would Verna *need* all three of those elements?

They had gone on in that vein for some time, pondering the places a person might be detained that would have access (or not) to elemental essentials. But they'd come up with nothing helpful.

Now she found herself lying in bed with no real sense of completion. She and Nina were going to head in a direction…but first they had to figure out what that direction would be.

Ten

The next time Verna slept after facing down Tod, she was surprised to feel the now-familiar sense of being watched. She opened her eyes and found herself looking into Tod's face once more. As he had the last time, he stood just outside the cell door, his back rod straight and his feet bare. Unlike the day before, his white feet contrasted not with the verdant greens and soothing purples of blooming thyme but with the brittle remains of dead leaves and broken stems.

She sat up, adjusting her robe over her bare legs and smoothing her hair down where it had grown a snarl while she slept.

"If you're about to ask me whether or not I think it's weird that you watch me while I sleep, I can tell you that yes, it's weird. Totally weird. Has it worked for you in the past? With former prisoners, I mean?"

If her impertinence caught him off guard, he didn't show it.

"No," he said without missing a beat.

"Ah. There's a saying about always doing the same thing and expecting a different result, isn't there?"

He continued to watch her but said, "That isn't what I meant. It hasn't worked with other prisoners because I've never had a prisoner before." His shoulders relaxed somewhat, and he looked around her room. "I actually wish you wouldn't call yourself that. You aren't a prisoner."

Verna snorted and then was annoyed to discover she was embarrassed at having snorted in front of him. She covered it up by getting suddenly and intensely mad at Tod.

She stood up, crossing her arms over her chest and striding across the cell with her eyes narrowed.

"Oh, really?" she asked, standing before him in a madder, less fecund version of the previous day's—night's?—tableau. "What do you call this, then? Hmm? Because kidnapping a person and holding her in a cell and not letting her leave seems like the exact definition of *keeping her prisoner*."

He rolled his eyes, and Verna's intense anger transformed into boiling rage. She wrapped her hands around the bars of the cell door and snarled through them, "You. Are. So. Lucky. You're lucky these bars are here, you milk-skinned bastard, because if they weren't, I'd climb you like a gecko and beat the snot out of you."

His expression darkened, and he moved a few inches closer to the bars. He was more than a head taller than she was, and his inclined forehead hovered a hair's breadth from the cold metal. "That's exactly the reason these bars are here, Verna. I knew you'd...," he paused, his expression changing from anger to puzzlement. "I'm sorry, but did you just say you'd climb me like a gecko?"

"Yeah. So? Why? What's your big objection to geckos?" Even in the midst of her anger she sensed her tone might be a bit too confrontational for a question about lizards.

"I don't have an objection to geckos," he said, backing away from the bars again. "It's just that so many other animals would make more sense in that threat."

Verna backed away from the bars and threw her hands up in disgust.

"Oh, I'm so sorry," she spat, drawing out the *so* to make sure Tod understood just how sorry she was. "I'm sure you could have picked any number of more vicious climbing animals to threaten someone with." She stood in the middle of her cell with her hands on her hips, glaring at him.

"Easily. A bear, maybe? A raccoon? A mandrill would be really terrifying. Or one of those monkeys that people keep as pets. They seem sweet, but then they turn on their owner and attack. What are they called?" he mumbled more to himself than to her. He rested a hand on his hip, looking off to the side as if the name of the adorable attacking monkey might be written on the stone wall.

"Capuchins? Sugar gliders?" Verna guessed.

"Sugar gliders are not monkeys," Tod said with a withering look.

"I'm pretty sure they are," Verna returned with venom, although as the words left her mouth her brain began working double time to fact check that claim.

"And *I'm* pretty sure they're marsupials. That hardly matters since the issue isn't taxonomy but threat potential. No one would cower at the thought of being set upon by a sugar glider."

Verna felt she might be losing the upper hand in this debate. "Someone with a fear of marsupials would be terrified."

"Ah-ha!" Tod nearly shouted, his body animating more than she'd yet seen it do. "So you admit they're not monkeys!"

"Damn it," Verna muttered. She strode back to the bars. "Who cares what they are? All of this is beside the point, which is that you're keeping me prisoner here, and I don't like it."

He dropped his head to look directly into her eyes, and she felt a frisson of disquiet at the depth of darkness she saw there.

"I don't like it either," Tod responded. His voice was calm and steady, and she sensed he meant it. "But I need you here, and I need you contained until I can figure out what to do next. I tried to figure out a way to do this that didn't involve holding you against your will, but this seemed like my only option. So, I did what I felt I had to—chimps!"

Verna reared back in surprise. "What?"

"Chimps. Those are the monkeys I was trying to think of."

Verna stared at Tod in silence, and Tod, to his credit, stared back unflinchingly.

Finally, Verna broke the silence. "Tod," she said coolly, "I think it's time you and I had a good, long talk."

Eleven

Coincidentally, Winnie awoke at the same time as Verna that day, although neither sister would ever know it. Her mouth felt cottony from the night before, and her eyes were stuck shut with sleep, but as wakefulness prodded her mind, the memory of the progress she and Nina had made the night before filled her with a rush of excitement. She sat up, cringing when her equilibrium took longer to make it into a sitting position than the rest of her body. Sunlight behind her curtains made them glow. It was going to be another beautiful summer day. In March. She sighed.

She shuffled to the bathroom to clean herself up for breakfast. She was distracted as she stepped into the shower, her mind turning over last night's conversation with Nina, so it was several minutes before she realized she smelled bacon cooking. Someone was in her kitchen. This wasn't particularly unusual: her sisters had keys to her apartment, and it was typical of them to let themselves in when she wasn't home to help themselves to her books or clothes or cupboard contents. This early and in this weather, Winnie was willing to bet Meri had come looking for a free breakfast.

Her hunch was confirmed a few minutes later when, wrapped in a robe and combing through her damp hair, she walked into her kitchen to find Meri at the stove in an apron, frying eggs and flipping bacon.

"Hiya, sis," she called brightly over her shoulder when she saw Winnie. "Is it okay if I make breakfast?"

Winnie snickered, pulling orange juice from the fridge. "I think it's too late for me to say no, Mer."

Meri spun, the dripping spatula clutched in her hand. "Would you have said no?"

Winnie clucked. "Of course not. What are we having?"

The two sisters settled down to share breakfast, and Winnie was once again glad for the distraction. Winnie found herself telling Meri about her evening with Nina, describing her job woes and her brisk, honest personality. Meri, who was always happy to share in all her sisters' joys, listened intently, exclaiming in just the right places and asking questions at every turn.

But when it came time to describe their conversation about Verna, Winnie found herself hesitant to mention it. What would Meri think about Winnie asking for help from a stranger? What would she say if Winnie told her she had revealed their true natures to Nina? And would Meri try to dissuade her from pursuing their plan? Winnie wasn't sure, and though it seemed something close to betrayal, she left off the end of the night's discussion. But thinking about it gave her another idea.

"I've been thinking a lot about the stuff we talked about at breakfast yesterday, Mer."

"The stuff about the croquette, you mean?" Meri asked around a mouthful of bacon.

"The crocus, yes. Maybe you and Autumn are right: maybe I should just wait and see what happens. I mean, I had the idea that I could track down Vee using that flower, but how would I even do that? I don't have any growth elemental: my elemental is all about slumber and dormancy. If she was going to send that message to anyone, she really would have sent it to you since you're the other growth Elemental. You'd know way better than I would how to track down where she was when she sent that flower, you know?"

Meri looked at her thoughtfully. "Oh, yeah. That would definitely make more sense." She stood and began moving toward the toaster. "Want more toast?"

Winnie screwed up her mouth as she studied her sister's back. "Sure, I'll have one more piece." She pondered for a moment, trying to figure out the best way to pick Meri's brain without her cottoning on. "They're such different magics. I really couldn't imagine how you two manage to grow things or track their origins. Do you need to do that even? Track a plant's origin, I mean."

Meri turned to face Winnie, leaning against the counter as she waited for the bread to toast. "Well, Vee really needs to do that more than I do since she's in charge of new plants coming up after winter ends. She has to make sure that the right kinds of plants are growing in the right places. It wouldn't do to have bromeliads sprouting up in Canada or something crazy like that. And she has to figure out things like late frosts and early showers. By the time I get involved, everything is growing. I have to worry about summer seeds, but those are mostly taken care of by birds and animals. So as long as I keep the weather right for them, the seed spreading happens."

"I see," Winnie responded, puzzling out how this information might be helpful. "So you wouldn't really know how to track down where the crocus was sent from either, I guess."

Meri set buttered toast on Winnie's plate and sat down beside her again. "No, not really. My elemental is pretty much all above ground."

"What about Autumn? She handles all the below ground dormancy. Maybe she'd know better than either you or I?"

Meri studied the chandelier, chewing slowly. Winnie watched her, recalling Autumn's irritation with Meri's slow mastication the day before and quashing the desire to urge her to hurry up. Meri worked in her own time.

"I doubt it. She puts everything to sleep, regardless of where it is. It wouldn't matter to her where it came from."

Winnie sighed deeply and then pulled herself together, remembering that she was trying to keep her decision to pursue the crocus a secret from her sister. She took a bite of toast and slumped back in her chair.

"Anyway, now that Autumn's not here to pooh-pooh, I can tell you about this perfectly delicious barista I've been seeing…"

And so it went for the rest of the morning: Meri regaled her sister with stories about barista Braydon and his perfect deliciousness while Winnie feigned both interest and attention, busying herself with cleaning up the mess Meri had made of her range and wracking her brains for a way to trace the crocus's origins. With the tiny part of her mind that was leftover, she just plain worried: what if there was no way to find her sister after all? And, what if Verna was lost somewhere, frightened and waiting for help that wasn't coming?

Twelve

Tod settled a three-legged stool amongst the shriveled thyme outside the cell and sat down. Verna found the sight to be somewhat ridiculous: the stool was too short, and his long legs stuck out bizarrely to either side, his knobby knees erect as mountain peaks.

"My first question for you would be why you killed the thyme when you were so keen to fight for it?"

Verna looked around at the sea of dead plant material. "I didn't kill it," she said sadly. "I can make it grow, but I can't make it thrive without sunlight. There's life in dirt, you know, but once it's used up, it's gone. It's like it holds on to a little bit of light, but not enough to keep it alive very long."

Tod studied her as she spoke, and Verna felt he was studying not just her but her words as well, moving them around in his mind, probing them for deceit.

He was silent for a few moments before saying, "I don't feel the life in dirt. I'm surrounded by it, and all I feel is death."

"Like I said," Verna replied tetchily. "There's not much life in it, but there was enough to make the thyme grow that you found so very irksome."

He grunted and looked down again at the floor. Tod's lackeys, whoever they were, had swept out the cell, gathering the dead material with bare hands and carting it out the far-off door she'd heard many times but couldn't see. But the floor outside the cell remained littered with desiccated remains.

"Irksome indeed," he mumbled without looking up.

Verna rolled her eyes. "Tod, why am I here? Why are you keeping me locked up?"

He looked at her, leaning forward to rest his forearms on his long thighs.

"I have a job for you, Verna. There's something I need you to do."

"I already have a job, Tod. And it's a pretty important one, you know. So, you might have to find someone else to take care of whatever little task you have in mind."

"It's not some little task!" Suddenly he was on his feet, clutching the bars of the cell.

But Verna moved just as quickly to stand and face him. "It doesn't matter to me, Tod. Big or small, it's definitely *your* problem, not mine. I have a season to get underway. You need to let me go."

"Your season has come and gone, Verna. Twice. And no one has missed it. So that's all the proof I need that I made the right decision to bring you here. I'm sorry that I had to do it the way that I did, but I thought that if I tried to approach you any other way, you'd reject me."

Verna snorted. Before she spoke, she cursed herself once again for making such a ridiculous sound in front of Tod. "Did you think kidnapping me would make me more sympathetic? That's pretty dumb, Tod."

He sagged and sat again. "I know. But like I said, I was desperate, and I didn't know what else to do." His voice, once cold, now sounded despondent.

It went against every principle in her, but Verna felt a sudden surge of the feeling she had just denied:

sympathy. The dark figure that had stood so straight before her cell when she'd grown the thyme was now crumpled and a bit pathetic. He'd run his long, white fingers through his hair so many times that it stood on end. His dark eyes gazed, unfocused, at the floor, and his slender, pale arms hung limply at his sides.

Verna straightened. This man had taken her against her will and had incarcerated her without any explanation. He had no right to her sympathy! He was categorically a bad man, and the circumstances that led him to this point should have no bearing whatsoever on her reaction to him. There was no mitigation, no rationalization, that she could accept for what he had done to her.

Yet, he didn't seem evil. He didn't seem bad. Verna warred with herself. He seemed broken and damaged, and despite her strong objection to being in the situation he'd put her in, she couldn't help wondering what compelled him to do something so…bizarre. Surely it was outside the norm even for someone as weird as Tod?

"Tod," Verna spoke quietly through the bars. "Just be honest with me, okay? Why am I here? What is it you think I can do for you? I'm not promising to help you, but I'm a lot more likely to if you're just honest with me."

Tod rose again and moved close to her. Her small hands tightened on the bars, and he enveloped them in his, holding tight to her tensed knuckles. Verna watched as they disappeared into his substantial grasp, and a wild thought registered that, at least for a few seconds, their skin was the same bloodless white.

"Verna," he whispered, his black eyes on her amber ones, "I need you to die."

Thirteen

By early afternoon, Winnie was tiring of Meri's gushing over barista Braydon, and she was also a bit tired of feeding her sister who, an hour after finishing a sizable breakfast, was already scrounging in the kitchen for a pre-lunch snack. Winnie had finally suggested hot sandwiches, and as Meri continued to prattle on about hand-holding and neck-nuzzling—Meri had never outgrown the knight in shining armor fantasy she'd picked up back when there were actual knights in actual armor, despite those knights smelling strongly of wet horse, body odor, and ale—Winnie had put together and broiled a sandwich, trimming it with lettuce and pickles before serving Meri. Winnie refused to buy tomatoes; last year's disrupted season had made the price of fresh produce skyrocket.

When the sandwich had been consumed and the lunch things tidied away, Meri, who had been hunched over her sketch pad since breakfast, chattering and drawing simultaneously, abruptly stood and announced her departure.

"Thanks for lunch, Win, and for letting me talk your ear off about Braydon. I've got to run. I have, like, a million things to do before Braydon takes me out for dinner."

Winnie was leaning awkwardly over to one side, her hip resting against the kitchen counter, trying to alleviate the cramp her overfull stomach was causing, and at the sound of the word *dinner* she released an involuntary *oof.* How Meri could be thinking of yet another meal after the two they had consumed in the last few hours was beyond Winnie, who was seriously considering a nap and then a bottle of wine.

Maybe she'd invite Nina up later to brainstorm. It seemed to Winnie that Nina had an uncanny ability to intuit not just answers but questions as well. If she didn't know the answer to something, she seemed to know the right question to ask to land upon it. So even if Winnie hadn't come up with any ideas during the day today, continuing to discuss the problem with her might yield good results. It wasn't Winnie's ideal solution: she'd prefer to have a clear sense of next steps. But for now, a good brainstorming session might be the best she could hope for.

Winnie walked with her sister to the front door of the apartment to pick up the mail that had been dropped through the slot. She gathered it up off the floor and rose to open the door for Meri.

"I'll call you tonight after my date, okay? To let you know how it went."

Winnie agreed to this as if she had real interest in the details of the date, as if she hadn't heard Meri's blow-by-blow of hundreds of dates in the past.

Meri hugged her sister, planting a kiss on her cheek before walking out the door. Winnie had nearly closed it behind her when Meri called out from the top of the stairs.

"Oh, Winnie! I almost forgot. Mom would know."

"Mom would know what?"

Meri grinned. "Where it came from. If that croque—flower was really a message from Vee, she'd have sent it to Mom. I mean, it couldn't have grown without water, right?"

Winnie closed her front door, leaned against it, and listened to Meri's footsteps retreating down the stairs. Her heart pounded. Her mother! Of course! Every drop of water under the earth and above it answered to Brooke, and no matter where the flower had originated, water would have to have been used to urge it into life. Winnie marveled that this hadn't occurred to her from the beginning.

But as she rested against the door, breathing deeply to master her racing pulse, a wave of panic overcame her. Of all the people she would choose to enlist for help, Brooke was at the very bottom of the list. She was determined that Verna had gone off alone, and her mind was as powerful and intractable as the mighty waters at her command. She could never tell her mother about the crocus or what she thought it meant. Brooke wouldn't just refuse to believe her; she'd be furious at her daughter's willful refusal to accept what Brooke felt was a perfectly reasonable explanation.

A sudden knock on the door she still leaned against startled her so badly she shrieked. Clutching her chest, she spun and pulled the door open. Nina stood on the other side, and with the sudden movement, she let out an involuntary shriek as well.

"Winnie! You scared me! Were you standing there waiting for me to knock?"

Winnie snickered. "Not exactly, but I was standing here at the door. My sister just left, and I guess I was sort of lost in thought." Winnie's eyes lit up. "Oh, Nina! I'm so glad you're here. I was going to call you to see if you wanted to come by again this afternoon."

Winnie stood aside to allow Nina to come into the apartment, and Nina headed straight to the kitchen and deposited an oilcloth tote bag on the kitchen counter.

"I was coming by to ask you the same thing. And I brought lunch. You haven't eaten, have you?" Nina asked as she pulled a tub of hummus and a bag of raw veggies from the tote.

Winnie grimaced, the waistband of her shorts still uncomfortably tight against her full stomach. "I'm not hungry, but stay and dig in. I've got something to tell you, and I want to know what you think."

Nina headed to the table with her food. Winnie was reaching into the fridge for the pitcher of iced tea when she heard Nina exclaim, "Oh, Winnie. This is beautiful! Meri must have been here, right?"

Winnie looked questioningly toward her friend, and Nina held up the page of sketch paper Meri must have left on the table for her.

"Oh!" Winnie breathed, standing beside Nina to admire the pencil drawing of a single crocus. Her chest tightened, and she swallowed hard. Nina slipped an arm around her and squeezed gently. Winnie reached for the drawing and carried it to her bookshelf, propping it carefully against the book spines on a high shelf. A thought occurred to her, and she took down the drawing again, turning it over. Meri had labeled it in pencil: "The Croquette." Winnie smiled and shook her head.

Behind her, Nina had spread out lunch on the table.

"Let's hear it. What did you want to tell me?" Nina asked around a mouthful of mini cucumber. She swallowed and went on before Winnie had the chance to speak. "I hope you've had better ideas than I have. I've been thinking and thinking since last night, but I just don't know enough about your magic to be very helpful."

"That's okay," Winnie responded, replacing the drawing on the shelf. "I couldn't think of anything either, but Meri came by this morning for breakfast...well, breakfast and lunch...and she said something that I think will help."

Nina sat upright, excitement making the color rise in her cheeks. "Can she track the crocus? Will she help us find Verna?"

Winnie's chest swelled with gratitude. It hadn't escaped her attention that Nina had said *us* rather than *you*. Even if Meri had volunteered to help Winnie after all, it was clear Nina still considered herself part of the plan. And Nina's excitement at the possibility of a lead was genuine. Winnie sent another little pulse of thanks into the universe for her fortuitous meeting with this woman.

"She can't track a flower, and I asked her if she thought our other sister, Autumn, might be able to, but their elementals don't work that way. By the time Meri gets involved in the seasonal change, the planting and growing are mostly done. She just manages sunshine and heat. When Autumn picks up where Meri leaves off, she only puts roots and bulbs to sleep, so it matters even less to her where plants come from and whether they're in the right place."

Nina's eyes were wide with attention, but she screwed up her mouth in puzzlement. "So, if they can't help us, who can?"

Winnie leaned back in her chair and sighed, running her fingers through her white-blond hair. "That's where it gets tricky. Meri said something that I really should have figured out on my own, but I think I just didn't want to even entertain the idea of having to take this route because it's going to be really rough." Winnie bit her lip.

"Winnie, whatever you're thinking, don't worry. We'll figure it out. What's the plan?"

"We have to ask my mom for help."

Nina brushed her bangs to the side and pushed up her glasses. In a hushed voice she said, "I should be scared right now, shouldn't I? I mean, if you guys are these huge, elemental forces, your mom must be crazy powerful, right? Is she…God?"

Winnie burst out laughing. "No, Nina, she's not God, although she might tell you otherwise if you ask her." Winnie rolled her eyes.

"So, what is she? I mean, who are the parents of the seasons?"

"She's water," Winnie said, standing to retrieve the iced tea from the refrigerator and refill their glasses. "She works with each of us in different ways, providing groundwater and moisture in the atmosphere. You asked me last night how I make snow, right?" As she talked, she turned on the faucet, letting cold water trickle into the sink. "My mother actually has a lot to do with that. She provides the water…" She paused to allow the water to run over her hand and then cupped it, collecting a palmful. She held it, dripping, at eye level. "I provide the cold."

Nina watched, transfixed, as a shiver ran visibly up Winnie's body from her feet to her fingertips. She brought her hand close to her lips and blew gently. Even in the warm air of the kitchen, Nina could see the frost in Winnie's breath, and she gasped in delight as ice crystals formed on Winnie's skin. When she turned her hand over, a tiny snowfall tumbled from her palm, melting even before it had the chance to touch the tile floor.

"Oh, Winnie. That's wonderful." Nina was a little breathless, and Winnie grinned at the approval. Rarely had she shared her power with anyone, and Nina's reaction delighted her.

Nina pushed up her glasses again and straightened purposefully. "Okay, so we need to go talk to your mom. How much does she know about each drop? Like, if we called her right now, would she know that you had just run the water in your kitchen?"

"Yes and no. She can't feel every drop of water all the time, but she could find out if she focused on it. It's a big job, being an Elemental. There's a lot of, well, element to keep track of at any given time. So, none of us feels everything our elements are up to every second of every day. Right now, my element is totally silent here, but there's snow and frozen life in other parts of the world, and I'm responsible for all of it. But much of what we do sort of carries on without us. There's snow in the Himalayas, but it's mostly over permafrost, so I don't have to do much to keep it frozen. It's only the areas of the globe that experience big seasonal changes that I have to keep on top of regularly.

"But if you asked me about activity in any of that permafrost, or if you wanted to know about snow storms in India, I'd just have to tap into my elemental to know what was happening there. My mother is the same: she won't know it off the top of her head, but she'll be able to find out."

"Winnie, this is great! All we have to do is go see your mom, and we'll know exactly where your sister is!"

Winnie sat down across from Nina, resting an elbow on the table and cradling her chin on her hand. "Right. About that…"

"You said last night that your mom's pretty determined to believe that Verna left on her own, right?"

Winnie sighed and raised her pale blonde, almost non-existent eyebrows in assent.

"But surely if we tell her about the crocus and just ask her to help, she'd be willing? What's the worst that could happen? We find out that it's just some kind of natural fluke and has nothing to do with Verna at all. I don't think that's likely, but I feel like any mother would jump at the chance to help find a lost child, even if she doesn't have a lot of hope it'll work. And if it does work, won't she be ecstatic that we've got a lead?"

"Maybe," Winnie conceded as Nina rose to clear the table and put the lunch leftovers away. "But it's also possible that she'll be so mad at me for pressing an issue she's already closed the door on that she'll kick us both out on our rears. Or, she may decide to humor us and look into it and find exactly where the message came from and then throw us out because knowing the message came from Verna doesn't necessarily mean it's a call for help."

"You mean you think she'll say Verna's just letting you know she's still out there somewhere and perfectly fine." It wasn't a question, and Winnie was relieved that Nina seemed to be grasping her mother's contrary nature quite easily.

"I think it's distinctly possible, yes. If there's one thing my mother doesn't like, it's to be proven wrong."

Nina stood with a hand on her hip, and Winnie recognized the same look she'd worn the night before as she worked through the relationship of the four sisters. She waited quietly: Nina had already proven that she might work slowly on a problem, but her solutions were exceptionally useful.

Finally, she spoke. "We're going to talk to your mom, Winnie." She brushed aside her bangs with renewed purpose. "But first, you're going to tell me all about her."

"All about my mother?" Winnie asked skeptically. "It will take a while. My mom is an ancient Elemental, Nina. She's had millions of years to perfect being...the way she is."

"That's okay. I have all afternoon to listen. And tomorrow morning, first thing, you and I are going to wherever your mother lives and not leaving until we know where that crocus came from."

Winnie stared at her friend for a few beats before drawing in a deep, resigned breath. "Okay. I'm in. But if we're going to do this tonight, Nina, I'm going to need to put a bottle of wine in the fridge."

Nina's face brightened, and she reached into the depths of the tote bag that stood forgotten on the floor beside the stove. "I'm glad you reminded me." She straightened and held up two wine bottles. "Chardonnay or pinot grigio?"

Winnie looked from one bottle to the other and grinned. "Yes."

Fourteen

It had taken them all of the previous afternoon, most of the evening, and both bottles of wine, but Nina had finally drawn from Winnie all she felt she needed to know about Brooke to be ready to face her. Winnie had gone to bed afterward nervous about the meeting that loomed the next day but also encouraged by Nina's approach. Nina's work history and her boisterous ambition might seem flighty, but there was nothing hurried about her prep work. She'd asked Winnie dozens of questions about Brooke: how had she raised the girls? What was her relationship like with each of them? How did she get along with Pete, whom she neither lived with nor spoke to with any regularity? Winnie had answered every question to the best of her ability, including as much detail as she could remember—which often wasn't much given how long it had been since she'd been a child—and as many specific examples as she could muster.

A few questions into their discussion, Nina had stopped Winnie and scurried out the door without explanation. Winnie marveled that she was becoming so inured to Nina's impulsivity that she likely would have been more surprised if Nina had calmly and reasonably explained her departure. She sat passively sipping her wine, waiting for her neighbor to return. Sure enough, within a few minutes, Nina swept back through the door in as much of a hurry as she'd departed and plopped back down in the overstuffed chair.

"Sorry," she'd said breathily. "I needed a notebook. I want to keep track of all this information so that I can look at it again before we walk into the lion's den." As she spoke, she opened a dogeared spiral notebook to a mostly blank page seemingly chosen at random and began furiously taking notes. Winnie had no idea what part of what she'd already said Nina was writing out, but she could see from her place on the sofa that the page was already partly covered with doodled curlicues and stick men.

Finally, Nina had looked up and motioned for Winnie to continue, but the wine had taken effect, and Winnie had largely lost the train of their conversation up to that point. So, they started with a new question, Nina probing Winnie about which sister Brooke seemed to favor. And the night had continued in that vein—question and answer, pauses and scribbles—until Nina had abruptly closed her notebook and proclaimed her research finished.

"I'm going home to look this over a few times, and then I'm turning in. You do the same, Winnie: go relax and get an early night. If your mom helps us tomorrow, and she gives us a good lead, I think we should begin following it right away, so we both need a good night's sleep. What time should we get underway in the morning? Oh! That reminds me that I never even asked where your mom lives! She's close by?"

"Yes, she's here in the city. Close enough to walk, really, but if you think we'll be starting out on…well, on whatever journey she puts us on, maybe we'll grab a cab. How about nine? Mom won't appreciate us coming any earlier than that, I suppose."

Nina had wrapped Winnie in a tight hug and squealed in her ear. "Oh, Winnie, I'm so excited. I'm excited to meet your mom, and I'm excited for you to be even this much closer to finding your sister." She stood back and smiled at Winnie before adding, "And, I'm excited to have decent strawberries again." She poked out her bottom lip as if she and strawberries had been torn asunder by parents who didn't understand their love. "I've missed them. So, so much."

Winnie had guffawed, and Nina had gathered her grocery tote and notebook and headed home to her own apartment.

Now Winnie stood anxiously on the front stoop of their building, waiting for Nina to come out so that they could get on the road. Nina had texted her before eight to make sure she was up and ready to go, and Winnie had appreciated the kick in the butt to get out of bed and get ready. She shared Nina's excitement from the night before, but Nina had the luxury of never having met Brooke. Fear had yet to temper her enthusiasm.

Winnie was rehearsing how she might broach the subject with Brooke when Nina popped out of the front door and burbled an excited greeting. She hopped down the steps and took off up the street, pausing to call out when she noticed Winnie wasn't following.

"Come on, slow poke!" she shouted up at Winnie. "I need coffee, and then we need to find your sister!"

Winnie chuckled in spite of her trepidation. She'd take a page out of Nina's book today and simply roll with the punches.

Half an hour later, the two women climbed out of a cab in front of a stately greystone rowhouse. Nina stood before the wrought iron gate that blocked off the modest concrete path up to the front door. Unlike its more subdued neighbors whose doors opened directly onto an uncovered stoop, the house they faced now had a dim, covered porch with a single wicker chair, cushion-less, angled into one corner. The house stretched upward three stories, and heavy drapes obscured every window facing the street.

"This is your mom's house?" Nina asked, her head tilted back to gaze up at the hipped roof dotted with dormers.

"Yep."

"Huh," Nina responded. "It's so…homey."

Winnie snorted. "Yeah, that's definitely Mom's intention."

The girls looked at one another. "Are you ready to do this?" Nina asked.

"Ready as I'll ever be."

Nina reached out and unlatched the gate, pushing it open and stepping aside to let Winnie walk through. Nina followed her up the steps to the door and stood beside Winnie as she pressed the doorbell.

A sonorous tone sounded deep inside the house, and several seconds passed silently. Winnie's determination to adopt Nina's devil-may-care attitude began to quail.

What if her mother was out? What if they'd hatched this plan and brainstormed all evening for nothing? She could scarcely imagine drumming up the courage to do this again tomorrow. But just as she prepared to turn to Nina to suggest they come back in a few hours to try again, the lock clicked, and the door swung open.

Against such a large, intimidating door, Brooke struck a notable contrast. She was a slight woman with a trim, wiry build. A flowy, white cotton dress that skimmed the contours of her figure revealed shoulders narrower than Meri's and hips narrower than Autumn's, but she was certainly closer to Autumn in height; the dress brushed the ankle straps of chic white espadrilles. Her hair was blond like Winnie's and Verna's, but darker than either daughter's. It hung to her waist in waves. Her sharp eyes, blue like the ocean, were set in a face that seemed both youthful and wise.

Winnie could feel Nina vibrating with excitement beside her.

"Hi, Mrs...uhh...Winnie's mom! I'm Nina." Nina thrust her hand forward toward the petite woman, whose eyes widened in surprise. "You don't look anything like I thought you'd look."

Brooke Harvester looked down at Nina's outstretched hand and waited one small beat before taking it. Winnie knew this little calculation of her mother's: she was a regal woman who would never show bad grace, even to a stranger, but she subverted those good manners in a hundred tiny ways with minute glances and nearly-imperceptible hesitations. Winnie suppressed a smile at the thought that Nina likely didn't catch the little snub, so without guile was she herself.

"Hello, Nina. How nice to make your acquaintance. Hello, Winter." Brooke cast a brief glance at her daughter, who mumbled "Hello, Mother" so faintly that Brooke could hardly be blamed for turning back to Nina before she'd even finished speaking. "I'm hesitant to ask, but how exactly did you expect me to look, Nina?"

"Oh, you look so young! You don't look like Winnie's mom at all. If I'd seen a picture of you with your daughters, I'd just assume there were five sisters instead of four."

Winnie gaped at Nina, her mouth hanging open. This sentence, while perhaps true—as an Elemental, Brooke wasn't subject to the aging pitfalls that plagued humans—was also patently trite and fawning. But that wasn't what had Winnie so nonplussed, for she had heard thousands of people over the centuries flatter her beautiful and powerful mother with similar phrases. What had Winnie agog was that, somehow, Nina had sounded completely sincere. When she came to her senses and snapped her mouth closed, she turned her attention to her mother, who was also looking intently at Nina, albeit without the slack jaw, a face her mother would never make even when confronted with a shock.

None of them spoke. And then Brooke did something that made Winnie's mouth drop open once more: she smiled. It wasn't the tight, polite smile Winnie had seen countless times before when her mother's good graces warred with her disdain for something a guest had said or done. It was a genuine smile, and it transformed her cold, beautiful features.

Who are you? And what have you done with my real mother? Winnie thought uncharitably as she gazed at the familiar face before her wearing an unfamiliar expression.

"Aren't you kind to say so? Please come in, Nina." Brooke pulled the door wide and stepped aside so that Nina could enter.

Brooke began to close it behind her when Nina turned suddenly and said, "Winnie, aren't you coming in?"

Brooke peeked around the edge of the door at her daughter, her eyebrows raised in surprise. "Winnie, I almost forgot you were out there! Why are you dawdling on the porch? You're letting all the cold air out."

And...she's back, Winnie thought, sighing with relief and entering the house.

Winnie and Nina sat on an upholstered silk settee with high ebony armrests and tufted cushions in Brooke's front room, drinking coffee Brooke had carried out on a tray. The settee didn't invite lounging, so both women sat upright, their adjacent knees bumping from time to time. When Brooke excused herself to the kitchen to retrieve a plate of Danishes for the girls, Nina had leaned toward Winnie and whisper-screamed "I can't believe your mom has a tray to serve coffee on! I feel like we're at Downton Abbey!" with a look on her face of such rapture that Winnie choked on the sip of coffee she'd just taken and had to accept a linen napkin from her mother, who had reentered the room just in time to see Winnie red-faced and spluttering into her elbow.

"Really, Winter. Slow down. You're too old to need a pat on the back," Brooke scolded.

She turned to pour her own coffee, and behind her back, Nina mouthed *sorry!* with a contrite grimace. Winnie kindly waved away her apology. Even without Nina's help, she would have managed to do something her mother disapproved of.

"So," Brooke said, settling herself in a high-backed chair across from the settee. "To what do I owe the pleasure of this unexpected visit? Winter, honey, how have you been? I hope you've been keeping track of Summer?"

"Yes, Mother. I just saw her yesterday, in fact. She came to my apartment for breakfast." She sipped her coffee before adding, "And lunch. And elevenses in between."

"Don't criticize. Summer is under a lot of pressure right now. I'm sure she's working around the clock to keep up with the added work she has."

Winnie thought of Meri's promise to text her with news about last night's date with the barista, a text that had yet to come through, perhaps because dinner had become breakfast as well. *Working around the clock indeed,* she thought.

Wisely, though, she said only, "I think she's keeping herself busy, Mother. But you know Meri: she finds plenty of ways to blow off steam." Winnie gazed down into her coffee to avoid her mother's studious gaze.

"Indeed," Brooke said with satisfaction, clearly confident that her third child had gotten this laudable attribute from her. "And what about you, Nina? What do you do for a living?"

Winnie cringed. Leave it to her mother to start with the one topic Nina had the least impressive response for. But once again, Nina surprised her friend.

"I'm working with Winnie, Mrs...uhh...," Nina faltered.

"Harvester," Brooke and Winnie provided simultaneously.

Brooke smiled again kindly and, at least to Winnie, disconcertingly. Maybe Nina had her own magic that she'd been keeping secret.

"But you should call me Brooke, Nina. I insist." She glanced from one girl to the other. "Now what do you mean when you say you're working for Winnie? What work could Winnie have for you to do?"

"Not *for* her, Mrs...I mean, Brooke. I'm working *with* her. We've partnered up on a project. We're actually neighbors, you see. I live right below Winnie. And we've become friends, and in the course of getting to know one another, something very exciting happened to Winnie, and she and I decided to tackle it together."

Winnie watched her mother's face anxiously. She'd run through half a dozen scenarios since the previous evening, imagining how she'd broach the subject with her mother and what she'd say in response to any number of different questions and challenges her mother might come up with. Most of her scenarios had ended with Brooke standing at the door, coldly insisting they leave and never bring up the subject of Verna's disappearance again, but in none of her possible scenarios had she imagined Nina taking the lead and explaining the situation to Brooke.

Brooke studied Nina's face intently, inscrutably placid. Her blue eyes took on a green tint in the diffuse light of the sitting room. She blinked infrequently. Under that gaze, Winnie had always felt compelled to speak and keep speaking, far past the point that she had exhausted her reserve of interesting things to say. But Nina didn't seem intimidated: she gazed sweetly back at Brooke, sipping her coffee and waiting politely for Brooke's conversational volley.

Brooke had been holding her coffee cup with one hand and its saucer with the other. She set the cup in the saucer and placed both on the claw-footed ebony table beside her.

"And what is this 'very exciting' thing that's happened to you, Winnie? I've heard nothing of it."

Winnie wondered if Nina could hear the ice in her mother's tone or if it was just the history of ice between them making her hyperalert to its presence. She hesitated, and Nina placed an encouraging hand on her wrist.

"Tell her, Winnie," she said earnestly. "I know this is something that's really hard to deal with, but your mom seems super cool. I know she's going to want to hear this."

Winnie swallowed, trying to reconcile the words *super cool* with the terrifying natural phenomenon that was presently gazing at her from across the regency sitting room. She took a deep breath. If Nina wasn't intimidated, she wasn't going to be either.

"Mom, I believe Verna has sent me a message."

Her mother's face hardened imperceptibly. Nina wouldn't have noticed it, but Winnie saw Brooke's eyes close ever so slightly and the faint lines around her mouth deepen with tension.

"I don't know what you're talking about, Winnie. And I'm sure Nina doesn't care to have our family matters monopolizing what could be an otherwise pleasant visit."

"Oh gosh, Mrs. Harvester...Brooke...don't worry at all about that! In fact, that's exactly why Winnie and I are here. You see, we've gone over everything we can together, but we've gotten to a place where we realized we have to bring in the big guns."

"Big guns?" Brooke repeated, enunciating the words as if she'd never heard them before and leaning back against her chair. She folded her slender arms over her modest chest.

If Nina caught the hint of contempt in Brooke's tone, she didn't let on.

"Absolutely. Winnie is amazing, Mrs. Harvester. What she can do—what all of the girls can do—is so incredible. Your daughter is powerful and intuitive and...well, just really special. I'm in awe of her."

Winnie felt heat creep up her neck from her collar. Could Nina really think all these things? More to the point, did she expect Brooke to agree with her?

"But when we put our heads together and really thought through the problem, we realized that all of that power and ability just wasn't enough. So naturally, we had to think bigger. Who would a powerful, supernatural being go to when her abilities were exhausted?"

Winnie reviewed the previous evening and was pretty certain their conversation had been substantially different from Nina's version of it, but she was beginning to see where Nina was headed, and a tiny spark of hope flared in her gut.

"It was so obvious: the source."

"The source?" Brooke repeated, but Winnie noted that her tone now was less contemptuous and more interested.

"Sure. The source of Winnie's power. And of Verna's too. The things they're able to do had to have come from somewhere, and that place is you, Mrs. Harvester. To have raised such amazing, resourceful, powerful daughters, you must be the most remarkable mother. So, naturally, we've come to you for help. Will you help us?"

Winnie held her breath. She could think of all kinds of words she'd used to describe her mother over the years, but none of them would have been useful in this discussion. Winnie realized that when it came down to it, Nina was right. She wasn't buttering up Brooke. At least, she wasn't doing *just* that. She had tapped into something that Winnie often overlooked: Brooke was, to her, just a mother, but to someone on the outside, someone like Nina, she was an imposing, terrifying, awe-inspiring force: a giver and taker of life. She wasn't just the source of Winnie and Verna and their myriad powers; she was the source of everything. She was The Source, capitalized.

Winnie studied her mother; she pondered the turbulent emotions certainly swirling under her unblinking mask. What did Brooke think about her daughter's disappearance when she lay alone in her bed each night? How had she worried and mourned? How many times had she swallowed anger and fear for the benefit of the three daughters who still relied on her, projecting the serene power they had drawn on year after year to promote and provide for the varied cycles of life that in turn relied on them? And how hard had Brooke worked to quash any germ of optimism about Vee's return for fear that it would only lead to greater disappointment down the line?

Brooke closed her eyes briefly and dropped her head. She heaved a sigh that forced her crossed arms off her chest and onto her lap. Then she straightened her back, clutched the arms of the chair, and said in a rich, strong voice, "Of course I'll help. What do you need from me?"

Fifteen

Winnie followed her mother down the hallway to the grand staircase. They hadn't seen much of the house when they'd first arrived; Brooke had directed them immediately from the petite vestibule inside the front door, through the house's interior doorway and foyer, and into the formal sitting room immediately to the right. Being a rowhouse, the home was narrow and deep. Now that they were moving farther into the house, Winnie could hear discreet noises of appreciation coming from Nina behind her. Dark-stained hardwood flooring directed visitors up the hallway toward a formal dining room on the right, a small kitchen with a pantry at the back straight ahead, or the sturdy stairway, its treads and risers carpeted in deep red, its carved newel post topped with a wrought iron finial, to the left. Nina clucked and cooed at the fleeting peek she got into the dining room, where a hexagonal table was already set and a crystal chandelier aligned perfectly with a fresh centerpiece: purple hydrangeas and lily grass in a clear glass vase stacked full of lemons and limes. The lack of spring, thought Winnie, had in no way altered her mother's taste in flowers, even if that meant she had to pay a king's ransom to have them imported.

They turned to head up the stairs, and Winnie noted the *ooh* as Nina glanced into the kitchen with its gleaming stainless-steel appliances and copper cookware prominently displayed around the pantry on wall hooks. She turned to Nina at the feel of her hand on the back of her arm, and Nina mouthed *Downton Abbey* again, her eyes wide with appreciation. Winnie stifled a snigger.

At the top of the stairs, they turned again into a short hallway and doubled back, reaching an identical stairway leading to the third floor. The doors in this hallway were closed, but Winnie could practically feel Nina forcibly overcoming her urge to open each one and poke around inside the concealed rooms.

At the top of the second staircase, they exited once again into a short hallway, and Winnie, whose anxiety about the meeting and subsequent relief at its outcome had left her feeling both fatigued and giddy, had the surreal thought that they had slipped into some kind of time loop and would continue to climb the same set of stairs, ending in the same hallway, forever. But her mother stopped halfway up the hall this time and looked up. The girls copied her pose, and Nina exclaimed over the rectangular trapdoor in the ceiling.

"Are we going into the attic?" she asked, her voice strained by the unusual angle of her neck.

"No. We're going through the attic. Winnie, fetch my step stool, please. It's just there, in the linen closet."

Winnie obeyed, and moments later they were on yet another set of stairs, this one having descended noiselessly from the back of the trap door. The girls followed Brooke once again, this time from the dim light of the hallway into the even-dimmer light of the attic.

Winnie had never been to her mother's font, although she had long suspected it was here in the attic.

The women in the Harvester family had been at their respective trades so long that they no longer involved themselves much in each other's magics. Winnie had seen the fonts at other homes her mother had inhabited over the years, but though Brooke had lived at this house for decades, Winnie had simply never had occasion to join her during the summoning of her power.

Now she blinked around the attic space they'd climbed into, searching for the basin her mother used to channel the power of her element when she had big magic brewing. But there was nothing particularly interesting about the attic space. The pitched roof forced the three women to the center of the space. At one end, one dormer window cast a pale light across the rough pine planks of the floor. At the other end, boxes sat stacked beside an old dresser and a wardrobe with peeling paint. For all Winnie knew, these items had been left behind by a previous owner.

So it was quite surprising to Winnie when her mother approached those boxes and began scaling them as if they were stairs no different from the ones they'd climbed from the ground floor. When she reached the top of the highest box, she stepped onto the dresser. Her head was now obscured in the shadowy depths of the attic's exposed beams. Winnie and Nina moved closer to peer up at Brooke.

To Winnie's amazement, following arm movements largely concealed from the view of the two onlookers, Brooke stepped up onto the top of the wardrobe.

Nina looked at Winnie in wonderment. "Winnie, did your mom just pass through the roof? Magically?"

Winnie quirked a brow at her new friend and chuckled at her astounded expression.

"No. She's an Elemental, Nina, not a wizard. She can't pass through solid objects."

"Oh, I know she's not a wizard," Nina responded, turning her gaze to the half-body visible below the rafters. "She's a woman. You have to call her a witch."

Muffled, Brooke's voice broke into their conversation. "I've been called that, or something very close to it, more than once in my lifetime, Nina dear." Her face reappeared suddenly as she bent to peek beneath the rafters at the girls. "But I have to say, no one's ever said it with quite your tone of reverence." She smiled conspiratorially at Nina.

Nina's eyes lit up. "Can I come up there with you, Brooke? Can you make my head…invisible, or…well, whatever you had to do to go through the ceiling?" She turned to Winnie with an almost manic grin. "This is so exciting, Winnie. It's like your mom is Mary Poppins!"

Brooke chortled with laughter at the comparison, and Winnie was thankful because it perfectly covered her own unflattering snort. "*Witch* was definitely more accurate," she murmured, but it was lost in the kerfuffle of Brooke's continued laughter and the sounds of Nina scrabbling up the boxes to join Brooke.

Winnie stared in disbelief at this: had she been too busy snarking to hear her mother agree to "magic" Nina's head through the ceiling? It had come as shock enough that Brooke hadn't batted an eye when Nina had revealed in the sitting room that she knew not only Winnie's true nature but her mother's as well. And now this? Perhaps Nina was the real witch here, casting an enchantment over Winnie's mother to make her understanding, sympathetic, and good-natured.

"Winnie, are you coming up here?" Nina's voice cut through her daydreaming.

"Yes, sorry. Is there room for all three of us?" She was already making her way up the pile of boxes, which she discovered were far sturdier than mere cardboard. The boxes themselves must house strong, wooden steps. It was a clever concealment, simple and effective.

Nina reached down to offer her a hand up to the top of the wardrobe, and though it was a tight fit, Winnie discovered as she straightened that all three of their heads had not passed magically through the roof at all.

"It's a cupola!" she exclaimed.

Her mother had reached up from her place on top of the dresser to move aside a panel concealed in the roofing underlay. Above it rose a square addition into which the upper half of all three women's bodies now squeezed. Its walls were louvered panels that permitted a breeze, although the space itself was oppressively warm. With all three of them breathing in the same small space now, Winnie hoped her mother's magic wouldn't take long.

"I needed a private place for my font, and I didn't want it underground in this house like I've had it in the past. But I was worried, what with the neighbors being so close, that they'd think it was strange if I was always climbing onto the roof. So, I had the cupola installed: it looks quite pretty from the outside, and I can collect water easily without anyone seeing me."

"Wow," breathed Nina, and Winnie saw that her friend was staring at her mother with unconcealed awe. "You really are a witch."

Brooke smiled coyly. "This is just the tip of the iceberg, Nina dear," she said.

Brooke reached above their heads to a round, soapstone basin that hung suspended from a single point at the top of the cupola. From that point, three brass chains supported a brass ring in which the basin rested.

"Is that your cauldron?" Nina asked.

"Nina, she's teasing you. She isn't really a witch. That's her font."

"Her what?"

Brooke carefully lifted the stone basin out of the ring in which it sat and lowered it so that the three of them could look into it. A small, serene puddle of water lay at its nadir. Winnie looked up at the brass hanger the basin had rested in. The cupola had a tiny hip roof similar to the greystone's. At the point where the four sides met, a decorative cap concealed a channel running the circumference of the apex, terminating in a small, brass spout. The spout was dry at the moment, but Nina imagined that when the air cooled at night, condensation would drip into the channel and run into the font. It wouldn't always be full, but Brooke didn't require font water to do all magic, just very powerful magic. And when a rainstorm blew through, the system was likely overwhelmed, and the font would overflow onto the door that Brooke had moved aside to access the cupola. But the gaps below the louvered panels told Winnie all she needed to know about where excess water drained off when the font was full. She had to hand it to her mother; it was an ingenious setup.

"This is my font, Nina," she spoke quietly into the small space. "This is where I gather rainwater or dew. It's a locus for my magic, a point of concentration for my powers."

She handed the font to Nina, who held it as if it were a holy relic, and carefully lowered herself back down onto the dresser. There was a fair amount of jostling and adjustment involved in this process since Winnie, the last to ascend, was closest to the dresser; therefore, the three of them had to shuffle clockwise to give Brooke access to the egress, Nina all the while focused intensely on the minuscule puddle in the bottom of the heavy stone bowl she held. As Winnie inched over to make space for her mother, it occurred to her how much easier this process would have been if she had simply volunteered to step out first and take the basin from Brooke once she was out, but the idea that her mother had handed the font to Nina and not to her rankled. She loved her mother, and Brooke loved her; surely it was childish to feel that, in spite of her love, her mother simply didn't have much faith in her.

Once the girls had climbed down, Nina having handed the font gingerly back to Brooke once the older woman was safely back on solid ground, Brooke nodded toward the wardrobe.

"Open those doors please, girls," she commanded.

Winnie moved to the wardrobe and tugged gently on the pulls. She'd expected the doors of such an apparently dilapidated piece of furniture to resist and creak, but to her surprise they swung open smoothly. Within, where Winnie might have expected moth-eaten clothing and cobwebs, a pristine marble pedestal stood on a polished wenge shelf inlaid with mother-of-pearl. Nina, looking over Winnie's shoulder, gasped.

"Oh, that's beautiful," she gushed.

"Slide it out, Winnie. This bowl is quite heavy."

Winnie pulled the shelf toward her, and it slid out silently. She stepped back and watched as her mother set the font carefully on the pedestal. She stood back and gazed at it, satisfaction infusing her expression.

"Stand back, girls," she instructed them calmly, and both Winnie and Nina obeyed instantly. Winnie glanced at Nina and felt sure from her expression that they were sensing the same change in the air. Brooke hadn't even begun summoning her magic, but the attic already felt cooler and damper. Water was gathering in the air around them, responding to the powerful magic that connected Brooke to her element without needing to be summoned.

Brooke breathed deeply and glanced from the basin to Winnie. "Are you ready, Winter?"

"Yes, Mother," Winnie breathed.

Brooke turned her gaze on Nina, and Nina's eyes widened. Brooke's eyes had looked blue initially, and later green, but now the irises swirled with color like eddies of ocean water in a turbulent cove.

"I'm ready, too," Nina said bravely. "What do you need us to do?"

"Tell me where the crocus is as specifically as you can."

"It's between two sidewalk sections in front of my building, Mom. Would a picture help?" Winnie had to raise her voice as she spoke because although they were in an enclosed attic, wind had begun to swirl around them. It began so faintly that she hadn't noticed it at first, hadn't noticed it, really, until it became the only thing she could focus on.

"Yes, let's see a picture," her mother answered without taking her eyes off the basin. She held her arms outstretched before her, as if she might step forward at any moment and grasp the sides of the font.

Winnie scrabbled in her shoulder bag to dig out her phone, pushing hair out of her eyes as her pale, choppy locks blew across her face in the swirling winds. She pulled up the picture she'd shown her sisters and held it above the basin where her mother could see it. Brooke's eyes narrowed briefly as she studied the picture; then, she nodded curtly and returned her gaze to the small puddle in the font, which had begun to vibrate and bubble in the turbulent energy of the attic.

Winnie tucked her phone back into her bag and took her place across from Nina, who herself stood at an angle to Brooke, watching the water simmer and biting her lip. Winnie caught her eye and offered a small smile. She mouthed *it's okay!* Nina smiled weakly, nodding to acknowledge Winnie's reassurance. The humidity in the air had dampened her bangs so that they clung to her temple, and sweat shone on her cheeks. She pushed up her glasses and glanced back at Brooke.

Brooke closed her stormy eyes and tilted her head back. Winnie felt magic tingle against her bare legs, and when she looked again at Nina, she could see goosebumps standing out on her upper arms. Nina was studying Brooke closely, but her attention was diverted suddenly by movement above the font.

Winnie wasn't afraid of what she saw; she was mesmerized. And when she glanced up at Nina, she was sure Nina felt the same way. The water in the font was…what *was* it doing? Winnie wondered. She cocked her head to one side to study the fascinating behavior of the water before her, struggling to put words to what she was seeing, even in her own mind.

"It's trickling up," Nina murmured, and Winnie grinned at her over the upside-down stream. That was precisely what it was doing: running from the basin up to the empty air above it in a gentle trickle. As it moved in apparent contradiction of gravity, Winnie was struck by another incongruity, but like before, Nina beat her to it. "And there's a lot more there than I remember being in the bowl."

"I've pulled it from the air," Brooke said, startling both girls. Her eyes were open now, and she was watching the reverse trickle with them, smiling in sweet appreciation of the element with which she was so closely connected.

"It's beautiful," Nina whispered, and Brooke's smile broadened.

"Thank you, Nina. Now we can find out what source fed your crocus, Winter."

She stared intently at the stream of water that hung above the basin, and Winnie felt another surge of power. The stream widened and grew, visibly pulling droplets of moisture from the wind as it whipped around them. As Winnie watched, the floating water formed a familiar shape.

"That's it, Mom. That's the crocus that's in front of my building." Winnie tamped down the excitement she was feeling, afraid of polluting her mother's magic with her own inadvertent surge or of jinxing her mother when they were so close to an answer.

"Let's see where you came from," whispered Brooke, and as she spoke, the crocus-shaped water blob, turning gently in the air before their faces, began to change, its watery roots lengthening as its petals seemed to drain away. Winnie watched, fascinated, as the roots split and spread in exponentially greater numbers until what they were looking at more closely resembled a smack of sea nettles floating in the ocean than the paths of water underground. Winnie felt a momentary vertigo at trying to reconcile the two discordant images: water in the air forming images of underground paths reminiscent of ocean jellyfish. She blinked several times to clear her vision and her mind.

Meanwhile, the water continued to split and bend and grow. Winnie became so disoriented by the sight that she had to look away. Nina's eyes darted from point to point, studying the image in parts rather than taking in the whole, and Winnie wondered if she was feeling as overwhelmed as Winnie herself was. But when she cast her gaze to her mother, Winnie saw serene appraisal. Despite her own impression of incomprehensibility, her mother seemed to be making cool sense of what they were seeing.

Then, just as Winnie felt she was reaching the breaking point from the heat of the attic, the moisture of the magic, the buffeting of the constant wind, and the chaos of the images swirling and mutating ever faster before her, everything froze. The water hung static in the air, rotating slowly as it had initially, but no longer growing or changing. The wind died away, and Winnie found the sudden, absolute silence as ponderous as the oppressive din of the gale had been.

She drew in a breath and held it, staring at the twisting mass of hair-thin lines that hovered over the font. The shape was vaguely spherical and so insubstantial that Winnie was reminded irrationally of cotton candy. She hoped her mother was making better sense of what they were looking at than she was.

But one look at her mother's face crushed her hopes. The serenity she'd seen there only moments before was replaced with confusion. Brooke had dropped her hands to her sides, and she was leaning forward, studying a point on the sphere with a furrowed brow. She turned her head this way and that, and Winnie could hear her muttering, though the chatter was too quiet to be understandable.

With a sigh, Brooke stepped back, and both Nina and Winnie jumped as the watery model splashed without ceremony back into the basin.

"Well, that's that," Brooke concluded.

"What's what?" Winnie asked, hearing the desperation in her voice and not caring. "What did you see, Mom? Could you tell where the water for the crocus came from?"

"Yes," Brooke answered, climbing back up onto the dresser and motioning for Nina to hand her the basin. Winnie could tell from the strain on her face as she lifted it that it was fuller now than it had been when they'd retrieved it.

"And?" Winnie demanded, although she was now talking only to her mother's bottom half. "Did Verna send it? Where did it come from?"

Brooke carefully climbed back down from the cupola opening, having fit the trapdoor back into place and checked that it was secure and watertight. She made to slide the pedestal shelf back into the wardrobe, but Winnie, fighting annoyance at how drawn out her mother was making this answer, took firm hold of Brooke's upper arm and turned her around to look into her face. Her eyes had returned to a sedate blue.

"Mom, please. What did you see?"

Brooke sighed deeply and put her hands on her hips. "I can't tell you for sure that your sister sent that flower, Winter." Winnie's heart sank, but her mother wasn't done talking. "But, there's something funny about where it did come from."

"Funny how?" Nina asked, moving to stand next to Winnie.

"It didn't come from anywhere I think you'd be able to get to easily. I mean," she went on in response to both girls' puzzled expressions, "it came from underground. Deep underground. But I don't see how anyone could be living as deeply as that map we were looking at suggested."

Winnie looked at Nina, who put a sympathetic hand on her back.

"What do we do next, Winnie? Can you think of any way we could figure out whether or not your sister is, like, living deep in the Earth?"

Winnie's head shot up, and she turned to look at her mother.

"Don't even look at me, Winter. You're going to have to talk to him, and you're going to have to do it without me."

Nina looked from one woman to the other. "I don't follow. Who's him? Who are we talking about?"

Winnie turned a smile on her friend. "To answer your question, Nina, yes we do have a way to figure out what's happening underground. And his name is Pete."

Sixteen

"I don't know why I let you talk me into this," Brooke said for the third—fourth?—time since they'd climbed into the cab in front of her graystone and pulled away from the curb. She was looking at Winnie as she asked it, but Winnie wanted to point out that, technically, she'd had nothing to do with convincing Brooke to join them on their trek to appeal to Pete; Nina had been the sole motivator, suggesting to Brooke that her cachet would go a long way toward coaxing Winnie's father to take up their cause, and another wise woman's input would only help to clarify and focus the information they received and the direction they went with it.

Typically, Winnie would have scoffed at this attempt to appeal to her mother's better nature—Brooke's nature was entirely one-dimensional, after all, and that nature tended toward things like typhoons and tsunamis—but once again Nina had worked her own magic on Brooke. After shockingly little convincing, Brooke had relented and excused herself to her boudoir to freshen up for the trip across town.

And so here they were, the three of them squeezed into the back of a taxi, with Brooke leaning forward to look past Nina in order to scold Winnie for Nina's actions. Winnie gazed out the front window and sighed.

"Let's think about a game plan. Don't you think we should?" Nina asked, and Winnie was glad for the distraction play. "How do you want to bring this up with your dad? What's his reaction likely to be?"

127

With Brooke sitting less than two feet away, Winnie couldn't answer honestly. What she'd like to have said to Nina is that Pete would be a completely different prospect from Brooke: flattery wouldn't work, nor would appealing to his sense of importance. Pete would most likely resist their request simply because he was both tender and oblivious. For being such a giant of a man, he had a remarkably soft heart, and centuries of experience had taught him that the best way to avoid getting hurt was simply to pretend the things that might hurt him didn't exist.

Which meant Brooke, the person who had hurt him the most for the longest time, was both the best and the absolute last person to bring along to see him. There was a reason the two past lovers kept that love in the past.

But of course, Nina would have no way of knowing this. In the hours she and Winnie had spent going over all the information Winnie could provide about Brooke and her relationship with each of her children, Pete's name had hardly come up. It hadn't occurred to Winnie when they were preparing for today that Nina would need any information about Pete because it hadn't occurred to Winnie that they'd end up in a hot, jerky taxi with Brooke, heading to see her estranged husband.

But now they were, and she struggled to think of any useful information to give Nina that wouldn't hurt her mother's feelings in the process.

"I think we should be forthright with Dad. He'll appreciate us not beating around the bush. But we shouldn't be blunt because Dad can be…"

"A crybaby," Brooke finished unsympathetically.

"Tenderhearted is the word I was going to use," Winnie corrected her mother without looking her way. She could feel Brooke's stare on the side of her face, and her cheeks became hot.

"Okay," Nina ventured, glancing from one woman to the other. "So, what you're saying is that your dad appreciates being informed about what's going on, but he also appreciates topics that are…delicate…being handled with regard to that delicacy. Does that sound about right?"

Brooke's cool gaze moved to Nina's face, and she raised one eyebrow. "Nina dear, I think I understand why Winnie let you do all the talking at my house this morning."

Winnie bristled. "Yes, Mother, and I'm sure you can also see why I think she should continue to do the talking when we get to Dad's."

Brooke's eyes narrowed; Winnie sat back in her seat and crossed her arms petulantly over her chest.

If Nina hadn't known it was meteorologically impossible at the moment, she'd have sworn the temperature in the cab dropped ten degrees.

"You know, it really is okay with me to take the lead on this. Winnie, I know you're emotionally taxed right now, and I'm sure it's hard for you to talk about this stuff. I'm sure I'd feel the same way if my brother was missing. And Brooke, we've already asked so much from you this morning, and you performed some pretty amazing…uh…"—she glanced at the back of the cab driver's head before continuing—"stuff back at the house, which I can only imagine takes a lot out of you. And I'm this third party who's seeing everything from the outside, so he won't feel like I've got some kind of agenda or something."

Winnie considered this. When she turned to tell Nina it was a good idea, she was surprised to see Brooke's hand patting Nina's. "Thank you, Nina. I think you're right. We really need you." Brooke said.

Nina grinned. "It's nice to be needed."

They pulled up in front of Pete's Rocks and Minerals, and the three of them disembarked, Nina pumping the front of her tank top open and closed like a bellows to get cool, and Brooke demurely dabbing at her upper lip with a handkerchief.

"I haven't been here in ages," she said, studying the water-spotted front windows displaying the backs of half a dozen shelving units. "I see your dad hasn't changed it much."

"No, not really," Winnie said. She glanced at her mother, whose expression put Winnie in mind of a child who has just had its first taste of a lemon wedge. "You know Dad's never been that interested in bringing in business."

"Your father has never been that interested in anything he couldn't mine, polish, or break with a hammer."

Winnie bristled again, but Nina laced her arm through Winnie's crooked elbow and gave her a reassuring smile.

"Families are funny, aren't they?" she asked Winnie too quietly for Brooke to hear. "They have all this baggage and infighting, but when push comes to shove, they can put all that aside to focus on one thing together. I feel really lucky that I get to be here to help you focus on finding Verna."

Winnie sighed. Nina was right: now was not the time to rise to her mother's bait. Brooke might want to dredge up old enmities, but she and Nina were here for one purpose only.

"Thanks, Nina. For being here to help and for keeping your cool when I'm really, really close to losing mine."

Nina grinned. "My pleasure."

"Did I say *really* close? Because I'm not sure I emphasized just how close I am to…"

"You did. Come on. Time to face your dad."

Nina pushed open the front door and stepped into the shop, holding the door open for Winnie and Brooke to pass through. After the bright sunlight, the three women stood in the still silence for a moment to allow their eyes to adjust. As they did, Nina began looking around. She leaned in to peer at the collection in the closest display, studying the tiny, bold script that labeled each chunk, flake, and polished orb. Pitted, black-speckled gabbro sat adjacent to pitted, black-speckled carbonatite. Nina looked from one to the other, but to her they seemed indistinguishable. On the next shelf sat a sparkling white specimen that looked to Nina like an overgrown chunk of salt. *Dolomite,* its card read, and Nina marveled that dolomite was an actual rock. Her pop culture references clearly didn't connect to legitimate geological study.

"Wow," she said, gazing at the cases containing hundreds of rock and mineral specimens. "I didn't realize there were so many different…you know…" she trailed off.

"Rocks?" Winnie finished, snickering.

Nina turned to her in complete seriousness. "Yes," she replied. "Rocks."

Winnie snorted, and her mother shot her a disapproving look.

"I promise I'll bring you back when this is all over, and you can look around. I'll even drag my dad out of his office, and he can go over the weight, type, and source of literally every single specimen in this place for you."

"Really?" Nina had the audacity to look thrilled by this prospect.

"Sure," Winnie replied, raking her fingers through her sweaty hair and thinking longingly of the cool corridor that led to her father's office. "I can't promise I'll join you, but I'll get you two started and check back in regularly over the course of several days to see if he's getting close to wrapping up."

Nina scowled, and Winnie chuckled, grasping her by the upper arms and turning her in the direction of the back of the shop. As Winnie moved her along, Nina said over her shoulder, "Winnie, did you know there's a rock over there called dolomite? When I hear that name, I always think of those old album covers with naked—"

"Ha, yes, Nina, that's definitely something we should discuss not in front of my mom, and also it's something you should not ask my dad about," Winnie voiced quietly through gritted teeth.

They'd reached the door to Pete's first office. Nina blushed and glanced at Brooke, who seemed, thankfully, to be distracted by the thick layer of dust on the closest display case. Nina caught Winnie's eye and winked.

"Gotcha," she said with a grin.

They headed into the first office, and Winnie breathed a sigh of relief that in the couple of days since she'd been here last, Pete hadn't had time to accumulate more debris. Thank goodness she'd taken the time that day to clear things up a little. Her mother would likely find plenty to complain about after today's visit; at least she wouldn't have the mess Winnie had walked in on last time to add to the list.

"It doesn't look like your dad is here," Nina observed, looking around the small office space. "Maybe we should have called ahead."

"He's here," Winnie assured her. "It's just that where he's at he doesn't get cell service."

Nina's eyes sparkled with sudden delight. "Oh my gosh, Winnie. Is your dad invisible?" Before Winnie could disabuse her of this idea, she began turning on the spot with her hands out, like a blindfolded child feeling around in the air for an elusive pinata. "Mr. Harvester? You can show yourself! My name is Nina, and I'm a friend of Winnie's!" Her words were overloud and slowly deliberate.

Brooke gaped at Nina, but Winnie stifled laughter. Winnie took a few deep breaths to collect herself. "Nina, my dad's not invisible."

Nina dropped her hands. "Oh. But you said he's here…"

"I didn't mean here in this room." Winnie had to stop again to giggle. "And even if he were, why on earth are you talking like that? He speaks English, and his hearing is just fine."

Nina looked thoughtful for a beat and then began to giggle too, and in much the same way they had the first time the two women had sat in Nina's kitchen, their giggles evolved into fits of laughter. Brooke fought to maintain composure, but the sight of the girls' unabashed merriment finally made her crack, and she covered her mouth demurely with her hand to stifle her laughter.

Winnie gasped for breath, clutching at a cramp in her side, and wiped her eyes. "Come on," she said, pulling aside a box crammed with other collapsed boxes that shielded from view the open trapdoor that led to Pete's real office. Winnie had bugged her father for years to close the door after himself; he rarely had customers, of course, but she'd worried about the possibility of someone coming into the shop unnoticed, finding the open trapdoor, and surprising Pete in a sensitive position. But Pete refused: he always heard the bell, he claimed, and he needed to sign for deliveries. Winnie knew this wasn't true at all: she'd gone to the post office hundreds of times for him with delivery notification slips in hand, struggling back under the weight of boxes that felt—and truly had been—full of rocks. And today, he clearly hadn't heard either the tinkling bell that had announced their arrival or the crows of laughter that had followed soon after.

Winnie knew the truth: her father didn't close the door after himself because he just wasn't in the habit of doing so, and until he had an urgent and compelling reason to change his habits, he wouldn't. Pete's nature was simply hard-headed.

Fortunately, her father had gotten good at concealing the trapdoor with accumulated clutter. This was likely a happy accident; the door could have been anywhere in the shop and it still would have been surrounded by disordered litter, but Winnie preferred to give him the benefit of the doubt and view this particular pile of junk as proof that he'd heard and validated her admonitions.

Nina, having managed to get herself under control, peeked over Winnie's shoulder at the open maw with its serrated tongue of rough stone steps.

"Is he down there?" she asked, excitement in her tone.

Winnie grinned at her. "Follow me."

Winnie led the two women down the stairs, thinking as she went that just a few days previous she'd descended these same steps in a state of hot anxiety and uncertainty, and now...well, she was still technically hot and anxious and uncertain but for a totally different and more hopeful reason. This could very well be the last step in locating Verna. If nothing else, that cast today's anxiety in a more positive light: she was anxious about doing something rather than about doing nothing.

Winnie's positive self-talk was interrupted by her mother's voice behind her. "I see your father hasn't changed anything down here, either."

They were nearly at the end of the passage: Pete's main office lay only a few feet ahead of them. As Brooke's voice faded away, a shuffling sound ahead announced Pete's whereabouts, and his imposing form moved hastily into the doorway.

Behind Winnie, Nina gasped audibly. She leaned in to whisper in Winnie's ear, "You didn't mention your dad is a giant!"

Winnie smiled. "Don't worry," she said. "He won't grind your bones to make his bread. If he wanted to kill you, he'd do it by boring you to death with a discussion of basalt." Nina stared at her. "Come on, Nina. I'll introduce you."

Pete stepped aside to make room for them to enter, and Winnie made introductions. Pete was polite, but his attention was clearly focused squarely on Brooke, who had greeted her husband cursorily and then proceeded to stroll around the space, scowling down at the tools and materials on his workbench like a potential housekeeper calculating what she'd charge if she took on this job.

"You look well, Brooke. It's been a long time, hasn't it?" he said kindly, his blush visible even in the uneven light from the haphazard, unshaded bulbs.

Brooke turned to look at him, offering a polite smile that made Winnie frown. "Hello, Pete. I am well, thank you."

The four of them stood awkwardly in the silence that ensued. Winnie looked uncertainly from her mother to her father, waiting for one of them to speak—for Brooke to make a dismissive comment about the mess or for Pete to ask why under earth she was in his workshop for the first time in decades—but it was Nina who chimed in instead.

"Mr. Harvester, you sure have a lot of rocks up there."

Pete, apparently having forgotten that Nina was even in the room, took his first good look at her. "Do you like rocks...uhh..."

"Nina," she filled in. "And I suppose I never really thought about them much, but I poked around in some of your displays upstairs. You know, I guess I never realized how many different kinds of rocks there are! And Winnie said you know just about everything there is to know about every one of them."

Pete's jade-green eyes lit up. "Well, I don't know about *everything*...but I do have a very interesting specimen that just came in. Come over here, Nina, and take a look at this."

Whatever it was that Pete wanted to show off, and whether or not Nina found it truly interesting, Winnie didn't hear. The moment Pete's back was turned, Brooke was at her side.

"Thank you for bringing her," she whispered in Winnie's ear. "She's really taking one for the team."

"Mother!" Winnie scolded. "She is not. You don't know that whatever Dad's showing her isn't genuinely interesting."

Brooke rested the tips of four graceful fingers on her cheek and stared at Winnie, one eyebrow lifting with comical sluggishness.

Winnie scowled. "All right, it's definitely not interesting, whatever it is. But Nina will just make herself interested. She's good with people."

"And that's why I'm thanking you for bringing her along, Winter."

"Honestly, Mom, it's probably more the other way around. I don't know that I'd be here if Nina hadn't pushed me to come to you."

"Why wouldn't you have come to me on your own?"

Winnie was surprised by the question, but she was more surprised that her mother sounded a bit...hurt? Could that be what she was hearing?

"Well," she said, feeling that she was treading into unexpectedly dangerous territory. "It's just that I asked..." She was about to say *Autumn and Meri if I should come to you, but they agreed that was a terrible idea.* But it occurred to her that not only would this likely hurt her mother's feelings, it wasn't really fair to her sisters. She was a grown woman; her sisters' opinions mattered to her, of course, but what they thought of something she decided to do was immaterial. She made her own decisions, or at least she liked to think she did. But perhaps she let her sisters' judgments weigh too heavily on those decisions. After all, Nina had evaluated all of the concerns she'd voiced, and she'd put them into perspective. And here they were now, benefitting from Brooke's invaluable advice.

"You asked...?" Brooke prompted her.

"Um, I asked myself if it was fair to get your hopes up. But Nina and I talked through it, and she suggested we'd all rather regret exhausting our options without success than regret not doing all we could when we had the chance to do it. And I think she was right."

Brooke squinted in appraisal. "Is that all, Winter?" she asked.

Winnie studied her shoes for a moment. "That's mostly all," she answered quietly.

"Mostly?" There was the vaguest hint of tenderness in her mother's voice, and Winnie looked up at her when she heard it.

Winnie found a rough place on her thumb nail and began biting it. "It's just that," she said around her finger, studying the spot she was worrying as she spoke. "It's just that I kind of thought..."

Brooke grabbed her daughter's hand and forced it back down to her side.

"Stop eating your finger and speak, Winter. You're behaving like a chastened child."

Winnie met her mother's gaze, stung. "Well to be honest, Mother, that's about how I feel. Like I'm a little girl you don't approve of. And frankly, I thought if I came to you and asked for your help, you'd say something like what you just said and make me feel dumb for even suggesting Vee might ask me for help. But I think she did, and I think the fact that we're here

139

now is proof that she has more faith in me than you do."

It was Brooke's turn to feel stung, and she clearly did, judging by the look on her face. The two women, mother and daughter, stood staring at one another, and it suddenly occurred to Winnie that the subdued drone of conversation from the other side of the workshop had stopped. She turned to see Pete and Nina watching her and Brooke. She looked from her father's expression of quizzical concern to Nina's apologetic grimace. *Sorry!* she mouthed.

Pete cleared his throat. "Ladies," he said in his rumbling baritone. "I think it's time you explain to me exactly what's going on."

Seventeen

The four of them sat squeezed around the three available sides of the table in the first office. They had explained the situation in detail to Pete: the crocus, the idea to track it, the trip to Brooke's. He had listened to it all grimly, sipping coffee with no sign of tasting it much less enjoying it. He'd interrupted only occasionally to ask clarifying questions, but otherwise he'd simply permitted the story to wash over him without apparent interest or surprise.

Now, they were quiet. In such close quarters, there should have been little opportunity for them to look anywhere but at one another. But Winnie was completely focused on the nail she'd now bitten down to the quick, Brooke was staring daggers at the top of Winnie's head, and Pete was studiously inspecting the popcorn ceiling as if he'd only just noticed it existed. Nina's gaze moved from one to the next to the next, waiting patiently for the heavy fug of discord to dissipate.

As the minutes ticked by, that seemed less and less likely to happen on its own. So she endeavored to help it along.

"Okay," she said, her voice sounding unusually loud in the prolonged silence. It seemed as though this couldn't possibly be the same room she and Winnie had filled with gales of laughter scarcely an hour previous. "We've all taken a few minutes to absorb some new...revelations."

Brooke snorted at the term and turned her head away in disgust. "That's one word for what I've just absorbed."

Winnie looked up at her mother's profile, her cheeks burning. She cast a glance at Nina, who smiled a small, sympathetic smile and squeezed Winnie's hand. Winnie swallowed a hard lump. Things had been going along so well, but her big mouth...Why had she let her mother get to her?

Nina took a deep breath and pushed her glasses up her nose. "I think what's really important right now is prioritizing the things that we can address first and table, at least for now, the things that can be dealt with after we've gotten Verna back safe and sound. It's clear from how emotional all three of you are that Verna is really important to this family, so I vote we set everything else aside and focus on that. Can we all agree to do that?"

Winnie answered first and without hesitation. "Yes. I agree. Dad?"

Pete seemed startled by the reminder of the three women sitting before him. "Well, I thought we'd agreed to let this go, Winnie," he said gruffly. "But your mother...I mean to say that if she came here in person...I suppose it must mean...?"

At the reference to her involvement, Brooke met her husband's eyes. Winnie held her breath. It would be so like her mother to stand up and simply walk out of the shop, leaving them to figure this out alone. If she did, Pete would almost surely crumble as well. Winnie loved her father dearly, but she wished he would stand up for himself. She felt a wave of guilt as soon as she thought it. What right did she have to think that about him when she was so incapable of doing it herself?

Winnie swallowed. She'd caused this mess. It wasn't her father's job to diffuse the tension, and it certainly wasn't Nina's. She and Brooke would have to address the enmity brewing between them, and the thought of doing so made Winnie cringe, but right now, that couldn't matter. She couldn't make Brooke see her point of view, and she couldn't change the reaction her mother might have to being defied, but she could put right what she'd put wrong today, and she could address the rest of it at a later time and in a better way. She turned to her mother.

"Mom, I'm sorry I said what I did. I was wrong. I want to talk more about it, but right now, I think Nina's right. Verna is why we're here. We need your help; you're essential to this process. Please, can we work together?"

For a moment, staring into Brooke's cool, appraising eyes, Winnie was sure she was going to walk away from the search for Verna. But with a wave of her hand, Brooke swept away the miasma of strain.

"Certainly," she said briskly. "I've come all the way across town already. We might as well see what your father can dig up."

"Ha!" Pete's sudden guffaw startled Winnie and Nina. "'Dig up'! Did you hear that, Winnie?" He leaned back in his folding chair, its joints squealing loudly in protest, and rapped the flimsy table with both hands.

"That was quite a good one, Brooker. 'Dig up,'" he repeated, chuckling so that his whole body shook.

With one hand, Nina reached up to Winnie's chin and closed her mouth for her.

"Yay!" she then cheered, sitting up straighter and brushing her bangs aside. "What do you need from us, Pete? Do you want Winnie and me to fetch your bowl?"

Pete raised an eyebrow in puzzlement. "My bowl?"

Winnie, having regained her senses, leaned into Nina to get her attention. "Dad doesn't use a font, Nina. Water isn't his thing, remember?"

Nina slapped her own forehead. "Of course," she said, grinning. Her eyes lit up. "It's something totally different, then?" She turned to Pete. "I can't wait to see your focus, Pete!"

"My what?" Pete was clearly struggling to follow the conversation.

Nina was about to repeat herself when Brooke cut in. "Locus, Nina dear. Not focus. Pete, I can tell you where the water that fed the crocus originated, but it's up to you to interpret what it means. Nina will help you fetch your locus. Winter, get me a glass of water while I touch up my makeup. We'll reconvene here at the table in five minutes." With that, Brooke excused herself to the restroom, the other three looking after her in silence.

"Is your locus underground?" Nina asked as Pete rinsed the coffee cups they'd been using and set them in the sink.

Pete looked at her thoughtfully. "I don't think so."

"What do you mean you don't think so, Dad?" Winnie asked from behind them. "You know where your locus is, don't you?"

Pete turned back to her and leaned against the front of the utility basin. "Well..." He scratched his stubbly chin with one massive hand. "I know it's here in the shop." He looked around, apparently hoping it might appear on command.

Winnie shot Nina a wide-eyed look.

"Okay," Nina said with the tone she had adopted repeatedly today, the one that said *someone has to focus on solutions rather than problems, and that someone is going to be me.* "We'll help you find it. This shop isn't that big...how hard can it be? What's it look like, Pete?"

"Gneiss."

Nina reached up to pat him tenderly on the arm. "Aww, I'm sure it's very nice. I mean, it's precious to you and central to who you are and your power...," she trailed off at the mystified look on Pete's face.

"Nina." Winnie was scrubbing her face with her hands, her chunky bangs standing out at angles. "Not 'nice'. Gneiss, with a g."

"I don't follow. Nice with a g? Wouldn't that be gice?"

"No, I...wait, what? Gice? That's not even a word."

Nina was just drawing in breath to respond when the door behind them opened, and Brooke joined them, asking "All set then? Pete, where's your locus? And my water?" She looked around to emphasize that despite her directions being exceedingly clear, all three of them had managed to fail at their assigned tasks.

"Mom, do you know where Dad's locus is?"

Brooke turned her formidable gaze on her husband, who hastened to stand up straight, his hands thrust into the pockets of his cargo pants and his eyes fixed on a point somewhere above his wife's head like a schoolboy caught shooting spitballs. He was so much taller than she that even looking over her head meant he was looking down a bit.

"Pete."

"I didn't lose it," he responded too quickly. Winnie couldn't help being impressed by how few words her parents needed to communicate with crystal clarity.

Brooke harrumphed. "Nina, follow me, please. Winter, that water?"

Brooke strode through the door to the front of the shop, Nina following close behind. When they were gone, Pete caught Winnie's eye and smiled sheepishly. Winnie tried to look stern, but the childlike expression on her father's ancient face melted her resolve.

"I love you, Dad," she whispered.

"I love you too, Win," he whispered back. "But you better get that water before she comes back."

Five minutes later, Brooke and Nina were back, and a decidedly mundane chunk of rock sat on the table around which the foursome now stood. It was squarish and rough-hewn, dark grey and shot through with thin white stripes. It looked a lot like a doorstop.

"He uses it as a doorstop," Brooke said, unimpressed.

"But a *nice* doorstop," Nina added quickly, smiling up at Pete.

Pete returned her smile kindly but turned to Winnie with a look that said *it's not just me, right?* Winnie looked away quickly to avoid snickering and endeavored to explain the confusion to Nina as soon as she had a piece of paper to write "gneiss" on.

"Are you ready, Pete?" Brooke asked, and Winnie pulled herself together to focus.

"You bet. It's been a long time since we held hands, Brooker," Pete responded, wrapping his paw around Brooke's delicate, outstretched hand.

Brooke gave him a disapproving look, but Winnie noticed that the corners of her mouth drew up ever so slightly. Brooke turned away from her husband and held her other hand over the glass of water Winnie had set beside the gneiss specimen.

"Here's what I found," she said, and as she spoke, the water in the glass rose upward.

Nina looked like she was bracing for an assault, but Winnie attempted to allay her concerns, saying, "Don't worry, Nina. This won't be like last time. Mom's just manipulating the water to show Dad a map. She's not drawing on the element, so it doesn't need the same level of magic. It'll be like what I did in the kitchen."

"Oh, gotcha. Okay. I'm ready." She relaxed visibly, and Winnie realized her mistake.

"But that's just my mom. When Dad starts…well, I guess it *will* be like last time."

"Hush, Winter. Let your father focus," Brooke scolded. She had drawn enough of the water from the glass to recreate the map she'd first accessed in her attic. It was a much smaller and less detailed version; only one of the many tendrils Winnie recalled from the first map remained.

That's the path to Verna, she thought.

Winnie gave Nina a reassuring nod, but she needn't have. Nina was already absorbed in Pete's growing energy.

Unlike Brooke, who had used both hands to pull together the water necessary to communicate her commands, Pete kept one hand interlocked with Brooke's and wrapped the other tightly around the gneiss. As Winnie watched, her father's powerful fingers began sinking into the impossibly hard stone. She caught movement from across the table and looked up to see Nina opening and closing her mouth repeatedly. She realized that the rushing sound she was hearing wasn't surrounding her as it had been at her mother's; rather, it was the sound of fluid in her ears, and when she copied Nina's action, her ears popped.

As Winnie refocused her attention on the gneiss, she noticed that the remaining water in the cup Brooke had drawn from vibrated just enough to form ripples in its surface. Watching them expand, she seemed to feel the vibration causing them. She realized, suddenly, she *could* feel the vibration. She was leaning against the table, but when she moved back so that she was no longer touching it, the vibration continued, making its way from the table to the floor and up through her feet.

Suddenly, the gneiss burst, bits of broken rock spraying across the table in a small arc. A few hit Winnie's arms as they flew, but they weren't travelling fast enough to hurt, and they fell to the floor harmlessly.

But they didn't stay put. As soon as the rock was in pieces, the fragments began skittering across the table and over the side, landing with the tap-tap of dropped dried beans. From there, they jumped and popped across the floor. They were joined by bits of broken rock that had shot willy-nilly through the small room, all headed for the trapdoor.

Winnie watched as, like iron filings pulled by a magnet, they jittered through the opening and down the stairs. When they were gone, the vibrations ceased, and silence settled on the room.

Nina looked at Winnie, who mouthed *wait* and smiled. Nina nodded, her glasses slipping farther down her nose.

Moments later, a faint sound began to rise from beyond the trapdoor. As it grew, the vibration returned, weak at first, but steadily growing, until the table itself jerked and jittered. The glass on it tipped and spilled, the water tracing an erratic pattern as the vibration spread it helter-skelter over the tabletop.

Winnie looked at her parents, and though they shook along with the rest of the room's contents, they were calm, her father smiling down affectionately at Brooke, who had turned just enough to know he was watching but not enough to look back. He was admiring her, and she was permitting his admiration, and Winnie felt her heart swell at the thought of the lifetimes they'd shared.

Her attention was drawn from them, though, by a sudden, whooshing eruption of rock from the trapdoor. The rushing sound resolved at the top of the stairs where rock that had scraped walls and steps and ceiling on the way up rose, unbound, into the air and began reassembling itself over the table. Bits of the broken gneiss were visible in the flow of rock, but so were fragments of limestone and shale. Pete could have named every grain of sand, but Winnie saw only an amalgam of material that the gneiss had brought up from the depths of Pete's caves. Chip by chip, the rock Pete drew from under the ground knitted itself together around the fragile water map that still floated before them. Winnie watched anxiously as the map grew and gained form, rock filling in the spaces around the delicate tendril of water before finally completing the outline of the structure that could be found at its source.

With the addition of a few straggling chips that flew from the trapdoor in a final spurt, the map was complete. Silence fell in the office as the four onlookers marveled at what they were seeing. Like Brooke's map, Pete's was round. Caverns and pits were visible here and there, inconsistent in size and shape. But at the tip of the water tendril, a different kind of space had been revealed.

Winnie's brow furrowed, and she looked at Pete. She gasped when she saw that his face had drained of blood, and his normally jovial features seemed drawn and hollow.

"Pete," her mother breathed, and Winnie saw that she, too, was staring in horror at the map. "It can't be."

"What?" Winnie demanded, well and truly frightened for the first time since the night they'd discovered Verna's apartment empty. "What is it, Dad? What do you see?"

Pete seemed to fold, and he sat down heavily on the folding chair behind him. When he broke contact with his wife's hand, the water around which the rock map had formed drained out its bottom, though the rock itself remained intact, rotating slowly as it floated.

Winnie moved around the table to Pete's side, kneeled, and slid an arm around his shoulder. She wanted an answer desperately, but she was afraid of anything that could frighten her father like this.

"Dad?" she said, moving to look into his still wan face. "Do you know where Verna is?"

He met her eyes and nodded. "Yes, I do."

"Where is she, Dad? Just tell me. I need to know."

He stared at her, and though his mouth worked, no sound came out.

"Winter." Brook's voice drew Winnie's attention. Her mother still stood beside the table, staring at the oddly square space in the map. She raised her finger. "She's there."

Winnie studied the gap. "Where is that, Mom? What's that empty space? It doesn't look natural."

"It's the Depths, Winter." Brooke's voice seemed to have been robbed of life.

Winnie's head shot round to stare at her mother. "No. No, that can't be right. She can't be there." She raised her hand to her mouth, staring at the dark cavern.

A hand on her arm startled her out of her shock. It was Nina.

"I'm sorry, Winnie. I can tell this is bad, but I don't understand what's happened." Nina's voice was muted, and she spoke close to Winnie's ear as if they were at a funeral and she didn't want to disturb the other mourners. "What are the Depths?"

Winnie's heart thudded in her chest, and she fought to catch her breath. She looked back at the spinning orb and then dropped her head and closed her eyes.

"It's where people go when they die, Nina."

Eighteen

The four of them were gathered once again around the flimsy table, four untouched cups of coffee before them. Pete and Brooke were dry-eyed and unmoving, each gazing in different directions, though under the table their knees touched. Winnie gazed down into her cup, occasionally wiping silent tears from her cheeks.

Nina was silent too, glancing up from time to time to check on the status of each family member. But her eyes were dry: she was waiting for the right time to interrupt the family's shock. Time passed, but the three of them seemed frozen by grief. Nina decided it was time to act.

She cleared her throat. Winnie looked up, but neither her father nor her mother acknowledged the interruption. Winnie's face was puffy and pale; red blotches stood out starkly around her eyes and mouth. Nina felt Winnie's grief deeply, but rather than stopping her from saying what she felt needed saying, it spurred her on. If this family had something to grieve, there would be time for that. But Nina wasn't convinced it was necessary quite yet.

"Winnie, I think we need to figure out where the crocus came from."

Brooke's head shot up. "What are you talking about?" she demanded, challenge in her tone.

"Nina, don't you understand what I told you? That crocus came from the Depths. It's a place of death." As Winnie spoke, a tear gathered weight on her lower lashes until it fell, overcome by its own mass.

"Yes, I understand all of that. It's like the afterlife," Nina responded. She pulled another paper towel off the roll that Pete had set before his daughter on the table and handed it to Winnie. "I just don't think that means we should stop now."

Brooke made a noise somewhere between a scoff and a sob and looked away.

"Nina…"

"Hear me out, Winnie. Brooke, Pete, you too. I can't imagine how hard this must be for you, and I'm not going to pretend to completely understand what the Depths are and why they're so scary, but from where I'm sitting, there's still a really important question we haven't answered."

"Which is?" Winnie sounded skeptical, but Nina noticed her tears had stopped.

"Well, we know the crocus came from the Depths, right? And we assume that the only being on the planet who could have sent it is Verna, right?"

Winnie nodded, comprehension beginning to dawn. "Yes. Right. So, if Verna really did send the crocus…"

Nina picked up Winnie's trailing thought. "And if the crocus came from the Depths, then Verna must be alive in the Depths."

Brooke coughed derisively. "Preposterous," she said. "She couldn't be. Elementals and Fundamentals do not mix."

"Fundamentals?" Nina looked from Brooke to Winnie for clarification.

"Fundamentals control all the things on Earth that are inevitable. Life and death stuff. They've existed as long as we have, and we've always carried on separately. They have their affairs, and we have ours."

"It's why I can't feel Verna even though she's underground," Pete added, speaking for the first time since his map had revealed the terrible response to their inquiries. "The realms of the Elementals and the Fundamentals are sacrosanct. I have no more involvement in the Depths than I do in making snow or assembling ocean currents."

"The Fundamentals are far more involved with humans than we are," Winnie continued. We deal with the natural world, and whether humans are impacted or not really doesn't matter to us. But Fundamentals are very focused on individual people and the courses of their lives."

"They're pains in ass," Brooke spat, startling Nina with her outburst.

"Mother..."

"Your mother's right, Win," Pete said. "They're prickly, demanding, self-centered..."

"They function on a much shorter timeline than we do, Nina." Winnie actually agreed with what her parents were saying, but she felt Nina would look for the redeeming qualities in anyone she met, including Fundamentals; she admired that and found herself wanting to emulate it.

"How so?" Nina adopted the pose Winnie had come to think of as her guileless curiosity stance. In it, she would absorb every bit of information the Harvesters provided like a sponge.

"They deal with humans, and humans…well, no offense, Nina, but humans have really short lives. They go through all this crazy stuff in a very small amount of time: being born and falling in love and fighting and dying…it's a lot." She looked at her parents, sitting across the table. "We've been around a long time, and the processes we set in motion can last millennia. So, Fundamentals tend to think we're callous and disengaged, and we sort of consider Fundamentals to be reactionary and short-sighted."

"It's hard to have perspective when the only thing you focus on are creatures that live and die in the blink of an eye." Pete had been looking at Winnie when he said this, but he seemed to realize immediately how insensitive he sounded. When he glanced at Nina, he blushed crimson. Nina's mouth had become an uncharacteristic hard line.

"As a short-lived creature myself, I guess I have the same perspective."

"I didn't mean to say…," Pete trailed off.

"It's okay, Pete. I get what you mean." Nina smiled kindly, and Winnie stroked her arm.

"I think what my dad means is that since Fundamentals are so involved with humans, they have a totally different set of priorities, and things they think are important are not the same things we think are important. So, we don't always see eye to eye with them."

"If I suggest we go and talk to these…Fundamentals…that wouldn't be possible?"

Winnie looked at her parents uncertainly. What she knew of Fundamentals, she knew from their stories of dealing with them. She and her sisters had little cause to get involved with any of the Other beings; Winnie wasn't even entirely sure how many there were or what forces they managed.

Brooke remained seated, clearly uninterested in entertaining the idea of appealing to the Fundamentals, but Pete seemed to consider it. Perhaps, Winnie thought, he felt bad for having suggested Nina and her ilk were insignificant, and he was anxious to make it up to her now. Whatever his motivation, Winnie was thankful he was still helping. Everything she'd been through in the last few days had told her she needed badly to rely on the people around her for help.

"No," Pete said finally. "No, I don't think we can do that."

Winnie was crestfallen. "Why not, Dad? What if that's the only way?"

"Winnie, the Fundamentals have no reason to help us. We don't do much to help their humans, and it's been a bone of contention for a long time. Even if we asked them for help with this, I can't think of any reason they'd agree."

"And more to the point," Brooke cut in unexpectedly, "if they find out Verna's gone missing, what's to stop them from using that against us? They'll see it as a vulnerability. They'll find a way to exploit it."

"Mother, this could be the only chance we have to find Verna!"

"It isn't going to work, Winter!" Brooke was on her feet now, her cheeks pink with anger. "Why would they help us? Would you help them if they came to you?"

Winnie was stung. "I'd like to think I would, yes."

"Well, I wouldn't. They're not like us, and they ought to be able to take care of themselves. Just like we're going to take care of ourselves. I'm not groveling. I won't go to a Fundamental and beg for help."

Winnie opened her mouth to respond, but Nina held up a hand to stop her. "I think your dad has something to say, Winnie. Maybe we should hear him out."

Winnie looked at her father, whose forehead was furrowed in concentration, highlighting the smooth roundness of his skull. "What are you thinking, Dad?"

"I agree with your mother: there's probably nothing to be gained by approaching the Fundamentals with this, and perhaps even quite a lot to be lost."

Brooke turned to her husband with a look of triumph.

"But," he went on as if he hadn't caught her look, "I think we still have an option. It's just…a dangerous one."

"I'm not afraid," Winnie croaked before she'd really considered whether she was afraid or not.

"You should be. The Depths have a boundary my magic doesn't cross, but that doesn't mean it couldn't. It could."

"You mean you could look in the Depths?" Nina asked.

"No. If I could, we would have seen it today in the map. But there's nothing stopping us from physically going there."

Winnie and Nina stared at him.

"You're saying you could go to the Depths and look for Verna?"

Brooke clutched his arm. "No. No to all of this. Pete, you can't go there. They will know you're there the minute you cross the threshold. It's too dangerous."

"You're right. They'd know *I* was there."

He looked at his daughter. "You're powerful, Winnie. All you girls are. But your mother's power and mine are different. Your mom and I can't go into the Depths; our presence there would be recognized immediately, and the results could be..." He paused, thinking of the right word.

"Not great?" Nina volunteered. Brooke's lips pinched a little tighter.

"That's one way of putting it," Pete conceded.

"What's going to happen if Winnie and I go there?" Nina asked, and Winnie felt a now-familiar surge of affection for her and her willingness to put herself in harm's way without hesitation for a friend.

"I don't know exactly. But if you're right and Verna really is there and sending messages, then at least we know you girls can pass into the Depths without apparent repercussions and with at least some access to your elements. If there were another way...," he trailed off once again, but Winnie had a sense that she and Nina were already thinking the same thing.

"Are you sure you're okay with this, Nina? I have no idea what we'll find down there or if we'll be able to deal with it when we find it. I can't promise to be able to keep you safe, but I promise you I'll do everything I can to make sure we both make it back in one piece."

"I know you will, Winnie." Nina's eyes shone with excitement, but when Winnie reached out and grabbed her hand, she could feel it shaking.

"Okay," she said with a trembling smile, turning her gaze on her father. "How do we get there, Dad?"

Nineteen

Nina and Winnie followed Pete's hulking form through a winding, underground passage. Winnie had seldom passed into any of the stone-walled tunnels that led off of Pete's underground workspace, and she'd certainly never been this deep before. The walls were damp and smelled of wet earth, and in the dim light cast by their flashlights, she could see the channel of trickling water that ran alongside their path and whose faint tinkling provided a constant soundtrack to their descent. She fanned herself absentmindedly as the air grew warmer and more oppressive.

Pete walked mostly hunched, though both Winnie and Nina had plenty of clearance and walked comfortably in a line behind him. Despite the underground darkness, Winnie could feel their descent: at times it seemed they followed a level path, but at other times she felt herself fighting to slow her own momentum as they moved deeper into the ground.

It was just the three of them, and mostly they made their way in silence. Pete picked their path carefully over the rough ground, occasionally turning them to the left or right to follow a branching tunnel that seemed to the girls to be identical to the one they had just left. Yet it was clear to them that Pete was following a map in his head, like a rabbit navigating a warren that would confound unwelcome visitors.

The unremarkable view had turned the girls' thoughts inward. Nina pondered the extraordinary events that had led her here, blazing a subterranean path to the realm of death. Winnie thought about her mother.

When the decision had been made back in the ground-level office that Winnie and Nina would undertake this journey together, Brooke was incensed. She had insisted they give up on this idea altogether, that she had been right all along about where Verna was and why she had gone. Winnie had tried to point out that, in light of the evidence they had amassed that day, that assertion no longer made sense, but Brooke had only turned a scathing glare on her.

"You've insisted from the very beginning that you were right and I was wrong about where Verna went, Winter," she'd fumed. "You've gone out of your way to defy me at every turn. And now you've recruited your father to help you in this fool's errand. I don't appreciate being undermined and schemed against like this."

Winnie had been so shocked by her mother's outburst that she'd been momentarily speechless. This seemed so profoundly unfair of Brooke, who wouldn't risk a thing by simply supporting their decision. Winnie hadn't asked her mother to accompany them and had no intention of doing so; what could it possibly cost her to offer them encouragement as they headed into the Depths rather than pick a fight?

All at once, Winnie's anger had flared. She loved her mother and rarely fought with her, and this wasn't simply because ignoring Brooke's sometimes-infuriating behavior was easier than engaging her in battle. Winnie genuinely respected her mother's power and grace; she respected the consistency of her millennia of channeling and managing her element. But the roiling emotions of the last few days—the thrill of finding the crocus, the stress of approaching her parents, the pain of learning where Verna really was—had taken their toll, and Winnie found this latest emotional affront overwhelming.

"You know what I don't appreciate, Mom?" Winnie had countered, and she'd been deeply and shamefully delighted when her mother's eyes had widened in shock that her normally easy-to-cow daughter was standing up for herself. "I don't appreciate that I'm focused on Verna and what she needs right now, and you're focused on how this affects you."

Silence had settled over the foursome. Winnie had bitten her lip, quashing the urge to apologize immediately. *I've been honest, and I've said something unkind but necessary,* she thought. Obeisance and contrition had characterized her relationship with her mother, but she found now that she didn't want to apologize for doing what she felt was right. She braced herself for her mother's vengeance, and though she couldn't drag her eyes from her mother's face to confirm it, she thought she felt her father move into a defensive posture to prepare for Brooke's assault.

But to Winnie's surprise, that assault never came. Her mother had stared at her, unmoving, for several seconds, and then she had drawn herself up, smoothed her already perfectly smooth hair, and turned her back on the three of them. She had stridden to the table where her purse lay, slung it over her arm calmly, and then purposefully walked out the door and into the shop. A beat later, they heard the bell over the door jangle as she exited.

Winnie had considered running after her, but when she glanced around at her father and Nina, she saw that neither of them was making any movement toward chasing Brooke down. In fact, neither of them seemed particularly concerned about the direction the conversation had gone, and when Pete began moving around the office and gathering up items the girls were likely to need on their journey, Nina had quietly excused herself to the bathroom, suggesting to Winnie as she left that she should grab water bottles from the office fridge.

Winnie had joined Pete in the search for supplies, digging out a handful of spare batteries for their flashlights, a pen knife with a battered plastic case, a half-empty jar of salted peanuts, and a plastic zippered baggie full of what Pete mysteriously referred to as oddments: wire ties from bread bags, mismatched buttons, the cracked rubber cap from the leg of a folding chair, and a dozen or so other bits and bobs of dubious use. Winnie began to sense that Pete's main concern wasn't really preparing the girls—who would even know how to prepare for something like this?— but rather *appearing* to prepare them, which Winnie still appreciated. It was unlikely any of this, with the exception of the peanuts and water, would do them any good where they were going, but it was nice to think that at the last minute, her father would be able to ask lovingly if they had everything they thought they'd need.

It was nice, too, that he provided this mindless task in the last few minutes before they set off as the lingering tension of Brooke's departure slowly dissipated and the realization of what they were setting off to do took its place. When they finally descended the stairs to his workspace, Winnie felt calmer and more ready.

But as they walked, she found it hard not to replay the brief fight she'd had with Brooke over and over in her mind. She disliked fighting in general, and a pestering concern that the unkind accusation she'd made might be the last thing she ever said to her mother took hold of her and refused to let go. She found herself gnawing her lip as she walked, wishing her cell phone worked so deep underground.

But of course, she mused, it's not as if her mother would be likely to accept a call from her right now anyway. And when she considered what she'd say if she could talk to Brooke, she was surprised to discover she didn't actually regret what she'd said. Should she?

She was just starting to replay the scene again with an alternate ending in which she took the high road and accepted that her mother could say what she wanted and she, Winnie, simply wouldn't let it get to her when Pete stopped so suddenly that she plowed into his broad, blocky back. Nina stopped abruptly on her heels as well, and Winnie swung around her light to smile at her, sure she'd been every bit as lost in her thoughts as Winnie had been.

"This is it," Pete said. "This is where you go in."

"Here?" Nina looked around at the blank stone walls. "There's no door."

"There will be when I make one." He set down the lantern he'd been carrying and turned up its glow to illuminate the section of passage they'd stopped in. The girls clicked off their flashlights, mindful of using up their batteries unnecessarily.

"I can't believe we're here already," Winnie lamented. "Somehow I thought we'd be walking a lot farther."

"There are some gaps in your education that your mom and I should have addressed, Winnie. I'm sorry now that we didn't explain the Fundamentals to you better, although I admit there are a lot of things about them, and the Depths too, that neither of us really understands very well either. But one thing I do know is that the Depths are kind of in one place and every place all at once."

Nina looked at him in puzzlement. "How is that possible?"

Pete shrugged. "I don't know. How is any of this possible? You're standing half a mile underground with a woman who makes snow and a guy who eats rocks." Nina stared at Pete with half disbelief and half rock-star admiration. Pete added, "All I know is that when people die, they pass right into the Depths from wherever they are even though the Depths themselves are contained in a pretty small area."

"So how do you know this is the way in?" Winnie asked.

"I don't know how to explain it, Win. It's just…thin here. I've come across hundreds of spots like this over the years. I just feel them and steer clear. This is the closest one to the workshop."

Nina chuckled. "Unreal. I mean, you couldn't write this stuff."

Pete folded his arms over his chest and leaned back on his heels, studying the wall like a man showing off a classic car he'd lovingly refurbished. "Yep, it's pretty mysterious. It's sort of like a really small room with a really giant door."

"So…what do we do now, Dad?"

"I'll open the way in, and you girls take it from there. I've never gone any closer than we are right now, so I really can't tell you what's waiting for you on the other side of this barrier." He paused, contemplating the rock. "Are you sure you girls have everything you need?"

Winnie smiled warmly, remembering how he'd added the oddments bag to the old backpack he'd filled for her aboveground. "Honestly, who knows? But we have the obvious stuff, Dad. Thanks for filling our bags."

"I love you, Winnie." His voice was gruff, and Winnie pondered the range of emotions he'd undergone today. Her father had woken this morning anticipating another day like thousands before, not the tumult of being told one daughter was alive but lost somewhere he couldn't reach her and another daughter was headed off on a journey he couldn't share with little more than wishful thinking to guide her.

"I love you too, Dad." Winnie wrapped her arms around her father, enjoying the crush of his massive hug and hoping fervently that before long she'd feel it again.

She pulled away and stepped back, and to her surprise, her father turned to Nina and embraced her as well. Nina wasn't much bigger than Winnie, and Winnie watched as Nina disappeared inside her father's bulky embrace in the same way she herself just had. She hadn't felt the urge to cry when she'd been the recipient of that embrace, but seeing Nina dwarfed by her father, it struck Winnie how strong her father was and how weak she and Nina seemed by comparison. She hadn't been that afraid up to this point, but she wondered now if that lack of fear came from her confidence in their ability to survive whatever they were about to face or from the eternal, reassuring presence of her powerful father. A painful lump formed in her throat, and she swallowed several times rapidly to tamp down a strong spurt of emotion.

Nina gave Pete a final squeeze, and the two separated. She turned back to Winnie and smiled reassuringly. "Let's go get your sister."

Pete turned to the wall, and the girls backed up a step on instinct. Laying both hands on the wall with fingers splayed, Pete closed his eyes and breathed deeply. After several seconds of brief silence, he murmured, "Crumble."

Tiny fissures formed in the rock around his hands and spread across its surface like cracks in the surface of icy water. Winnie thought wildly of her mother's water map, how she had thought of sea nettles as she watched the root pattern growing. Now, the spreading cracks reminded her of the tangle of roots drawn in water above her mother's font. Fleetingly, Winnie longed for her mother's company, for the comfort of her mother's power and will. But before she could dwell on that idea, the cracking subsided, and with a noise like a sigh, the wall gave way and fell in a rocky heap at Pete's feet.

He stepped to the side, and the girls moved forward to peer into the hole he had created. Before them, a pitch-black maw spread outward from their point of ingress. And then, as they watched, a single dot of light began to glow in the dark depths. As the girls peered at it, the point of light began to grow. Winnie thought objectively that it resembled an oncoming train, and in another equally objective part of her mind, it occurred to her that she should be afraid, that under normal circumstances, looking directly into the light of an oncoming train should be terrifying, yet she felt no terror whatsoever. In fact, nothing about the situation seemed even remotely frightening to her. Frankly, her brain increasingly insisted, what would make the most sense right now would be to explore the light, to learn more about it. She should walk toward it. She was definitely going to walk toward it.

She had just lifted her foot to take her first step when she noticed movement to her right. Nina was one step ahead of her, literally: she had taken her first tentative step toward the light. Winnie reached out and grabbed her hand; when Nina looked back, she was smiling.

"We should totally walk toward that light," she said.

"I was just thinking the same thing."

And they did.

Behind them, Pete watched through the doorway as the two women, hand-in-hand, walked into what appeared to him to be intense and complete darkness. He was a being equipped with supernatural abilities to see in the dark, but even his remarkable vision revealed nothing.

"Turn on your flashlights, girls," he called to them, but the girls not only left their unlit flashlights hanging loosely at their sides, they didn't even acknowledge his suggestion.

"Winnie," he called. She continued moving away from him. "Winnie!" He was dismayed that she didn't turn, didn't even call "hang on" or "just a sec" over her shoulder. When he called a third time, louder, he realized something unsettling: his voice wasn't echoing inside the cavernous space that was, step by step, swallowing the girls.

He placed his hands on the rock on either side of the opening he'd created and watched helplessly as Winnie and Nina took the last few steps illuminated by the lantern in the passage and then vanished into the shadows. Then, he snatched up the lantern and raced as fast as his lumbering form could manage back up the winding corridors to the rock shop.

Twenty

Winnie and Nina moved closer to the light, and the light, it seemed, moved closer to them as well, growing in both size and brightness as they walked. Winnie had the surreal feeling of being both in her body and out of it simultaneously. She was very aware of her circumstances: she could feel Nina's hand in hers; she could feel the firmness of ground beneath her feet; she could recall the reality of having walked through the door into a space reserved exclusively for the dead. Yet at the same time, she seemed detached from that reality: shouldn't she be afraid of this light that ought to be blinding in the complete blackness but wasn't? Shouldn't she be afraid that she couldn't see the walls or ceiling of the space they were in, let alone hear or see anyone else who might be sharing it with them? Shouldn't she look back over her shoulder and make sure the door was still behind them so that they'd know how to get out of here when this was all over?

Ineffably, the answer to all of these questions seemed to be a tacit *no*. She wasn't afraid, she wasn't unsure, and she wasn't concerned about getting out. She just felt strongly that approaching the light was exactly what they should be doing.

And suddenly, it was time to stop. As if on command, she and Nina ceased to move. They turned to look at one another.

"No farther," Nina said to her, and Winnie nodded in agreement. She was unsurprised to see that Nina's face was serene, lit from one side by the light whose source they'd finally found.

When they turned to look at it again, they were no longer looking at a diffuse light but rather at a doorway. No door hung in the frame; it was simply a white stone archway suffused with light.

"I'll go first, okay?" Nina volunteered, and Winnie nodded assent. "But I'll keep hold of your hand."

Turning back to the doorway, she stepped through, her arm stretched out behind her to keep Winnie's hand firmly grasped, and then Winnie stepped through behind her.

"Oh..." Nina stood with her mouth agape, staring into the far distance.

Winnie stepped beside her, their backs to the doorway, and looked out in the same direction as Nina, but whether or not the two of them registered the same details was impossible to tell. Winnie stopped breathing as she looked out at the incomprehensible vision before her. Spread out around them, for as far as either of them could see, lay a brilliant expanse of...

"Everything. It's everything, Winnie. Everything is just...everywhere. I don't even know where to look. That's a rainforest."

"Where?" Winnie searched in the direction she thought Nina was looking, but her eyes seemed not to want to settle on any one sight.

"There," Nina responded, pointing. "See that big sandy area? A desert, I guess? Right in the middle of it."

"By the river?"

"River? Oh! I didn't notice a river. Where does it start?" Nina shaded her eyes with her hand rather comically, Winnie felt, since they were standing in what seemed to be broad daylight, yet there was no sun visible from which her eyes might need shading.

"It's too far in the distance to see where it's coming from." Winnie traced the river for as long as she could, but she came to a point where she could see no farther, far off in the distance behind them.

She realized she was looking in exactly the opposite direction from Nina; she'd turned a half-circle in her attempt to follow the winding path of the water, but that meant…

"Nina, the doorway is gone."

Nina looked at her and then spun to face the same direction. They had stepped through the doorway only moments before, but where it once stood, another overwhelming expanse stretched away from them, as unrelenting and varied as the view they'd stepped out to face initially.

"Winnie, is this…I mean, when people die, do they…" Nina couldn't find words to encapsulate the flurry of ideas and images swirling in her mind. "What is this place?"

"I usually tell people it's a waystation."

Both women whirled around at the sound of an unfamiliar voice. Behind them stood a man, his wiry black hair standing out in tufts around a gleaming bald patch and his drooping eyes mostly obscured by heavy lids above and dark rings below. A burgundy tunic draped his diminutive form, hanging nearly to his knees under a black, open-front hooded poncho. The hood fell slack down his back. Straight-legged trousers of nearly the same color as the tunic brushed the tops of his bare feet. Wiry hairs eerily similar to the ones on his head sprouted from his toes.

True to form, Nina was the first of the women to speak. "Hi there. I'm Nina Ramirez," she announced, stepping forward to close the space between herself and the newcomer and thrusting out a hand in greeting.

The stranger studied her hand for a moment before gripping it. "Abel Miller. Welcome." He turned to Winnie expectantly.

"Winnie Harvester," she volunteered, reaching out to shake Abel's hand. "If you don't mind me asking, Mr. Miller, where are you welcoming us to exactly?"

"I'm welcoming you to the next step in your journey." His voice was a bored monotone, the kind of voice servers use when reciting, once again, the available beverage options. "You've moved from the world you've known up to this point, the world you were born into, to this place, the world we all must pass through before moving on to our next grand adventure."

The girls looked at him blankly.

"You died," he said. "We aren't really supposed to put it like that, but to be truthful, it's easier for most people when I just come right out with it. You died, and this is what happens to everybody when they die."

"So…this is heaven?" Nina asked.

"If heaven is the concept of afterlife that you find most comforting and familiar, then you can certainly think of it using that term." Abel delivered this sentence as if he were reading a cue card.

Nina snickered. "I guess I'm not the first person to ask that, huh? How many times have you had to repeat that sentence in your life?"

Abel looked at her sardonically. "Literally not even once. Ask me how many times I've said it in my death, though."

Nina flushed, and her hands flew to her mouth. "Oh my gosh. I'm so sorry, Abel."

Abel shrugged. "Don't worry about it. I've heard it all at this point. Actually, you two are handling the transition better than a lot of people do.

Nina turned to Winnie and raised a palm. "Go us," she said, and before Winnie had the time to think about whether or not it was entirely appropriate, she high-fived her.

Abel stared at them. The girls stared back. The silence that settled among them seemed to stretch on and on.

Finally, Abel spoke. "I guess I lied," he said, looking back and forth between the two women, his drooping eyes pulled unexpectedly wide by his raised brows. "I *thought* I'd heard it all. You two are…interesting."

"That's one word for us," Winnie muttered, and Nina elbowed her.

"So, Abel, if this isn't heaven, what is it?" Nina asked.

Abel settled himself on a jutting boulder, and Winnie, surprised that she hadn't noticed the giant rock there before now, looked around and registered that they were actually at the top of a grassy hill dotted with rocks partially obscured by fuzzy moss. *Did it look like this when we came through the doorway?* she wondered, turning again to survey the landscape in all directions, searching for other new additions that hadn't been there moments before. But as she turned, she discovered that she couldn't quite remember what she'd seen the last time she'd looked around. She vaguely remembered there'd been a river—or a large lake?—but now when she peered into the distance behind Abel, she saw a broad sandy beach and ocean stretching far into a foggy distance. Had that been there before?

She realized Abel was speaking.

"…for them, this place is kind of what they expect to see, but that depends largely on what kind of person you were in life."

"I'm sorry," Winnie interrupted. "Can you go through that again? I got distracted."

Abel heaved a put-upon sigh that reminded Winnie of her mother in its calculated lack of subtlety. "I was just saying that this is the step between life and the end of life. People call it limbo or heaven or bardo or, I don't know, Valhalla, but it's really more like a waystation. So, when people come here, they see whatever they believed they'd see when they were alive. It looks a little different for everyone, and part of what you see depends on the person you were in life."

Fascinated, Winnie sat down beside Abel. "You're saying," she clarified, "that Nina and I are standing here next to each other, but we're seeing two totally different things?"

"Basically. People who imagined clouds and angels see clouds and angels." He cleared his throat uncomfortably. "Of course, the opposite will be true for people who believe something else awaited them."

Nina gazed around the landscape. "Winnie, what color is your sky?"

"Blue. Why?"

"Mine's blue too. When you look around, do you see water and trees and sandy patches and...villages and stuff."

Winnie looked around again, thinking about how she'd describe what she was seeing. "Yes, that's pretty much what I see, too. It doesn't feel like a real place because it seems like it's changing when I'm not looking, but it looks a lot like what you're describing."

"Maybe we're seeing the same thing because we're still alive."

Abel's eyebrows shot up, elongating his hangdog features. "What do you mean *still alive*?"

Winnie stood and strode purposefully toward Nina, taking her by the arm and pulling her a few steps away from Abel. In an urgent whisper, she said, "What are you doing? Are you going to talk to this guy? We don't know anything about him! We have no idea if we can trust him. What if he raises an alarm? What if he tries to hurt us?"

Both women looked over their shoulders at Abel who, still seated, was digging his right pinky deep into his ear with the look of a man gloriously unconcerned by the whispered goings-on of certain persons in his vicinity.

"Yeah, I don't think Abel's a threat, Winnie. Anyway, what option do we have? Look at this place! It's huge. Huge! On our own, how would we ever find Verna?"

"I agree, but I was thinking we could get him to help us without coming right out and telling him what we're doing."

"How?" Nina asked curiously.

"Well, we could just say that…I mean maybe we tell him we're…Okay, I haven't figured that part out yet."

"Hear me out, Winnie. This nice man is here to meet people like us—well, deader than us, but basically like you and me—to meet people who have never been here and help them find their way. That means he must have a pretty good idea about how this place works and how to get around it. If we're honest with him and just tell him why we're here and what we're doing, I really think he'd at least point us in the right direction."

Winnie peered at her friend skeptically, but she had to admit Nina had a point. Chewing her lip, she looked back at Abel, who had apparently given up probing the depths of his ear to study the bottom of his foot with intensity, scratching at a spot and examining whatever he'd managed to transfer from his sole to his fingertip with near-scientific exactitude.

"Eww," Nina murmured. "We shook that hand."

Winnie giggled, and Nina grinned conspiratorially.

"Come on, Winnie. We've come this far."

"You trust people so easily, Nina. You just see good things when you look at people, don't you?"

"Yes," Nina answered. "Because I hope they see good in me. Let's go see what Abel found in his ear canal."

Twenty-One

As Abel led the way down the hill, Nina and Winnie filled him in on why they had come through the doorway despite the obvious complication of not being dead. Winnie was relieved that Nina provided few specific details, leaving out Winnie's true nature and who exactly they were looking for and explaining only that they had reason to believe someone they cared for had ended up here accidently and seemed to have sent a distress call they were there to answer. If any part of it shocked him, he gave no hint, but at one point he asked Nina if he could touch her again, just to see if he noticed the difference in how she felt now that he knew she wasn't dead. Winnie coughed to cover the burst of laughter that erupted from her at the memory of Nina's comment about having shaken Abel's hand, but Nina gamely offered her arm for his inspection. He poked her exposed flesh a couple of times with one finger, but he turned away and continued down the path with nothing more than a shrug.

The moss at the top of the hill where they'd come through had given way to scrub, and then to sparse trees, and then to fairly thick forest, but they finally rounded a bend and the forest abruptly ended.

"Oh, what an adorable little town," Nina gushed as they came into a cozy village with thatched-roofed rowhouses lining both sides of the narrow, hardpack dirt street. "Do people live here?"

"If this is their ideal, yes. I suppose this is heaven for some," Abel responded with a tone that suggested it certainly wouldn't be his idea of heaven.

His disdain for other people's heaven made Winnie curious. "What's your ideal, Abel? How did you end up…umm…becoming a tour guide?"

Abel stopped abruptly and turned to look at Winnie, drawing himself up to his full height. The effect was diminished somewhat by the fact that he was several inches shorter than Winnie, and she herself was quite petite.

"As a newcomer, I'll overlook the impertinence of that question. Every person's ideal is highly personal, and many essences choose to spend their duration in solitude without sharing that information."

"Please forgive me, Abel. Of course. It's none of my business how you, er, essences spend your…"

"Duration," he supplied.

Winnie smiled sheepishly, but her apology seemed sufficient. Abel shrugged, turned, and continued to walk, leading them up the lane of the storybook village to its green. More quaint structures surrounded the green, and for the first time since their arrival, the newcomers found themselves face-to-face with other people.

"I'm not really a *tour guide*, you know," he said, over-enunciating the term with scorn. They had stopped to observe the comings and goings of other essences on the green. "My official title is steward. It's my job to make sure new intakes understand where they are and what their roles will be for their durations. And I'm a level two steward, which means I end up bringing most of my intakes to places like this village."

Winnie and Nina looked around curiously. Although there were people moving in every direction, the green could hardly be considered crowded.

"Everyone is wearing the same thing," Nina observed, and Winnie was surprised to discover that Nina was right but she, Winnie, hadn't noticed it. Without exception, every form she saw wore the same clothing as Abel in variously subdued colors, although from what she could see, none wore the loose-hanging poncho he wore open over his tunic.

Abel turned to look at Nina. "You haven't looked down, then?"

"Winnie! Look at us!" Nina was staring down at herself in shock, and Winnie, disbelieving, gawped at her own shapeless tunic and straight-legged pants.

"How could our clothes have changed without us noticing?" Winnie wondered aloud, but Abel only shrugged again.

"Everyone has a body still because no one knows what else to be, but the body you had in life is still back there. Well, I guess that's not the case for you two in particular, but for everyone else here, they're in bodies basically out of habit. They don't need clothing, but they expect it. So they have it. And apparently, so do you."

Winnie crossed her arms over her chest, feeling for the first time the weight of where they were and its deeply alien nature. She still felt no fear, yet the thought that her own body was being impacted in ways she not only didn't understand but apparently didn't even notice unsettled her.

Nina, of course, was delighted. "This is amazing, Abel! I never felt a thing."

Abel smirked as if this were a design element he himself had come up with. "Well, feelings in general are seated in the body. I guess you're subject to the same laws as everyone here who has actually died. At least as far as your body is concerned."

Winnie, who still stood looking out across the green, noticed something she hadn't previously. "What's that, Abel? That pool in the center of the green. People, er...essences keep stopping by it and looking in."

"That's an anchor pool. It's what keeps these essences here."

Winnie turned a quizzical gaze on him. "What do you mean?"

"Everyone you see here is anchored to a living person. Anchor pools let them see the person they're anchored to."

Both women gazed at the pool in silence. Winnie heard Nina swallow hard.

"Can we go closer?" Nina asked.

Abel grunted. "We can go closer, but it would be best if you didn't look into the pool itself. This isn't your place, which means this isn't your pool."

Abel moved ahead of them again, and the girls followed him. Winnie's eyes were riveted on the pool. It was a shallow circle, built up out of the ground with stone bricks, standing perhaps half a foot high. The stout wall containing the water was wide enough to stand or sit on, though perhaps not comfortably, yet no one did either; rather, the forms moving around its perimeter simply stopped and stood by its edge, gazing down into its serene depths.

The threesome stopped close enough to the pool to see the faces of the figures that surrounded it but far enough away that they saw the surface of the still water as only a reflective glint below the lip of the stone ring. Winnie studied the faces of the essences that approached the pool. They stepped up to the edge and stared fixedly at the water. After a moment, their faces softened, and Winnie imagined that must be the moment their anchor came into view. Some essences stood for several minutes, simply gazing at the water; others seemed to find whom they were looking for and turn away quickly, moving from the edge of the pool with a look of contentment so that another searching figure could take their place.

Occasionally, an essence's face changed from soft recognition to concern, and it occurred to Winnie that some of the anchors these people were connecting with must themselves be unhappy back in life. The essences who became saddened when looking into the pool lingered longest, standing at the edge for long stretches with their gazes glued to the unmoving water below them. They said nothing, and aside from the changing expressions on their faces, they didn't move.

Winnie was about to ask Abel more about the pool when one figure caught her attention. A woman who looked to be close in age to Winnie—though, she noticed, most of the essences appeared to be of a similar age, so perhaps one died at the age they had felt most vigorous in life—moved to the edge of the pool. Her expression changed quickly to one of deep concern, her brow furrowed with worry and her hands clasped over her chest. To Winnie's surprise, tears began to course down the woman's cheeks. Winnie glanced at Nina to see if she had noticed the same figure, and sure enough, Nina's attention was focused on the woman's face as well.

"Abel, what's happening?" Nina whispered.

"We can't choose what we see in the pool." He spoke casually, clearly accustomed to witnessing this kind of event and explaining it to newcomers, but he spoke softly and without his previous insouciance. "Mostly life just carries on, and essences can peek in and confirm that all is well. But sometimes…"

"All *isn't* well," Winnie finished for him.

As the three onlookers watched, the woman dropped to her knees on the stone wall. Winnie longed to step closer, burning with curiosity to see what the woman stared at so fixedly. But simultaneously she sensed that doing so would be a violation; she would no more try to see this woman's anchor and share the grief that was connecting them than she would climb into a stranger's bathtub or eat food left on an adjacent table in a restaurant.

The woman was now kneeling on the small stone barrier and leaning out over the water. One hand held firmly onto the stone, but with the other, she gingerly reached out a finger and touched the surface of the water. Her finger penetrated its motionless surface without causing a ripple. The other spirits surrounding the pool made no attempt to stop her, yet all movement among them ceased: no one stepped away, and no new essences approached. They all simply waited, still and silent, in the fullness of death.

Winnie found she was holding her breath. She exhaled slowly, feeling as firmly frozen in place as the rest of the spectators.

The crying woman's tears fell into the pool below her, and she slowly withdrew her finger. She sat back on her heels, her hands on her thighs. To Winnie's surprise, she was no longer crying; in fact, she looked serene. As Winnie stared, the woman looked up and met her eyes. Winnie felt her mouth drop open as the woman's form seemed to waver like a mirage and fade away.

Nina whipped around to face Abel. "What just happened, Abel?" There was panic in her voice.

But Abel seemed undisturbed by this sensational sight. "She faded," he said with another shrug.

Winnie quashed a strong impulse to grab Abel by his overly expressive shoulders and shake him. *We saw that for ourselves, you hairy-toed twerp!* she wanted to shout. She took a deep breath to get a handle on herself.

"We saw that for ourselves, you hairy-toed twerp," she said.

"Winnie!" Nina gasped, and Winnie slapped her hands over her mouth in horror.

"Oh, Abel, I'm so sorry I said that! I don't know where that came from..." Winnie's cheeks burned with embarrassment. What was happening to her? She'd

186

contravened Autumn's instructions not to do anything rash, dressed down her mother back at her father's shop, and now was being unconscionably rude to this virtual stranger who was the only help they had here in the Depths.

But to her surprise, Abel only snickered. "Ahh…that's better."

"What do you mean?" Nina asked him.

"Most people don't handle dying very well. I'm a lot more used to irrational abuse and unpleasant outbursts than I am to high-fives."

Winnie stared at him in disbelief, but there was no denying he seemed somehow lighter now that she had disparaged his podiatric hirsutism. Maybe listening to her gut and acting on its impulses wasn't such a bad idea.

"Follow me," Abel instructed as he turned and walked away, his bony form topped by his bare, bobbing head. "This isn't where we're staying. I'll explain more as we go."

Once they were on the road headed back out of the village, Nina prompted Abel to continue his explanation. Winnie was still too embarrassed by her outburst to say anything, and so while Nina and Abel walked side-by-side, she lingered behind them, saying nothing but listening closely as Abel spoke.

"Don't worry about what you saw back there. Anchor pools are primarily one-way: they exist so that we can see our anchors. But sometimes, when the circumstances are dire, we can use them to reach out to the people we're connected to."

"You're talking about…haunting?"

Abel looked taken aback. "Certainly not. Hauntings don't happen in the normal course of things, and level twos don't engage in that type of behavior. I'm talking about the essence sending a sense of comfort to his or her anchor. Back in life, people say things like 'I feel like my mom is standing here beside me' or something like that. And in a way, she is. That happens when the dead connect with the living they're anchored to."

"But why did she disappear?" Nina asked.

"It takes a lot out of us, so much that, for a while afterward, we just cease to exist."

"So, she'll come back?"

"Eventually. We don't do it often because we miss a lot."

"You mean you miss a lot of what's going on in the anchor's life?" Nina sounded as if she herself had been harmed by this phenomenon. "That's so sad."

"How much time will she miss? That lady back there?" Winnie's curiosity had finally overridden her embarrassment, and she jogged to catch up with the other two.

"There's no way to know for sure. It could be a few weeks in living time. If it took enough of her spirit, it could be years. That's why we don't do it more often."

"Because you might miss your anchor's whole life?" Nina turned to study Abel's profile.

Abel stopped and turned to face her. "No. Because we might miss their death."

Winnie sensed the weight of this pronouncement, but something essential to its importance escaped her.

"What happens if you miss your anchor's death, Abel?" Winnie moved so that she could see both of their faces. For the first time, she saw real emotion in Abel's expression. "Our anchors keep us here, in this realm. But as I told you when you first came through the door, this is just a waystation. We meet our anchors again when they pass over. We help our anchors find their anchors, and then...well, then they let us go. We finally get to pass on."

"And if you're not here waiting when your anchor dies?"

"Then we're nowhere. We can't come back here, and we can't pass on. We're just...gone."

"Oh," Nina lamented. "Oh, that's so sad." Nina studied Abel's face. "What happens after this, Abel? If this is a waystation, what are you—I mean we—on the way to?"

Abel suddenly smiled coyly, an expression that seemed unsettlingly out of place on his dour features.

"You're still alive, Nina. I assume you plan to stay that way after we've tracked down this person you're looking for?" The women nodded in agreement. "I'm happy to share the details you'll learn when you pass over for real, but what happens after this is a secret you'll have to wait to learn when you come back here. Whenever that may be."

Nina grinned at him. "Deal." She threaded her arm through his and marched off again, Abel shuffling for a few steps before regaining his footing and falling into hesitant step beside her.

Winnie followed obediently, looking suspiciously at the back of Nina's head. When she glanced at Abel's profile, she saw that he too was looking at Nina with an unruly eyebrow quirked in suspicion.

"Somehow I thought you'd fight that answer a little harder," he said to her.

"Oh, no. I'm perfectly happy not to find out all the secrets of this place," she chirped. "I'm just pleased you've agreed to help us."

Abel stopped short, and Winnie trod on the back of his bare heels.

"Jeez. Sorry, Abel."

Abel didn't seem to notice, so involved was he in gaping at Nina. "I did no such thing."

Nina turned her innocent, quintessential-Nina gaze on him. "You just said you're going to help us track down the person we're looking for."

"Well, yes. I mean I have to. That's what I do...I steward people. I meet them at the door they enter through and help them find the essence they're anchored to. I can't leave my charges until they've found the person they're looking for, so I have to help you find your person. But after that, you're on your own."

Nina's smile faded. "You won't help us rescue her? Get her back where she belongs?"

"No." Abel turned from Nina and continued walking.

"Abel! Wait!" Nina called as she and Winnie jogged to catch up with him. "Reconsider? We could really use your help."

"I learned the hard way not to cross the powers that be," Abel called back over his shoulder. "I'm doing this job to get out of the hole I dug myself into. I'm not risking the good credit I've earned to help a couple of *living* ladies." He spat out the word "living" as if it had four letters. "No offense," he called back lamely.

"Abel, hold up," Nina said, finally snagging him by the arm and spinning him around to face them. "What do you mean? What hole?"

Abel dropped his gaze, clearly reluctant to continue the conversation.

"Hey," Nina said consolingly, stroking Abel's scrawny arm. "Talk to us. We're asking a lot from you, I know, but maybe we can help each other."

Winnie shot Nina a look of alarm. What help could they be to this spirit they hardly knew? And, Winnie would have been embarrassed to admit, hardly liked? How much time might they end up wasting by helping Abel when they were supposed to be looking for Verna? She tried to catch Nina's eye, but Nina was entirely focused on the glum face before her. Winnie opened her mouth to interrupt, but as she watched Nina comforting Abel, she realized how out of line she'd be to do so. After all, the only reason Nina was here with her now, the only reason she'd been able to take any of the steps she'd taken in the last few days, was because Nina had happened across her at her very lowest and had offered, without thought for the peril involved or the personal cost, to help. Verna had waited this long: what harm could there be in just learning Abel's story?

"Nina's right, Abel," she said, drawing their attention. "If there's something Nina and I can do to help you, we will. You've already explained more to us about this place than we possibly could have figured out on our own."

Abel considered her, and finally he seemed to give up the last defense he'd been holding onto. "I suppose it wouldn't hurt to explain my position," he relented.

"That's the spirit," Nina said with genuine enthusiasm. "Tell us how you ended up a steward for the dearly departed."

"The answer to that can be summed up in one word," he said grimly, turning to walk off and staring straight ahead as Winnie fell into place beside him. "Tod."

Twenty-Two

Winnie caught Nina's eye behind Abel's back. Abel's tone suggested the name 'Tod' should fill them with dread, but Nina seemed as unaffected by it as Winnie felt. Abel, however, didn't seem to notice the lack of response from the women flanking him, and he carried on with his story as if the mention of his nemesis's name had struck the ideal tone.

"I've shown you ladies only level two essences," he began, and Winnie bit her tongue before the new, gutsy side of her could ask if he meant *living* ladies. "They're the most common type. They're people who are neither very good nor very bad in life."

"So just normal people?"

"Sure, that's a way to think of them. They don't really mean to do any harm, but sometimes they do anyway. Level twos."

"What are level ones? Like, priests and stuff?" Nina watched Abel's profile as he considered this.

"Yes and no. Level ones are people who are uniquely good, but being a priest doesn't have much to do with it. Some people who never step in any kind of church in life are level ones because they simply believed in doing for others, not because a religion told them to, but because their nature did. Level ones aren't my department, so I can't tell you much about their path when they come here, but they don't stay long. They get to pass on pretty quickly.

But to answer your question, plenty of people who might be considered religious in life end up here as level threes. The designation isn't made based on what you pretended to be or told people you were when you were alive. It's based on what your true intention was, on what resided deep inside the secret recesses of your living psyche."

"That's pretty deep, Abel," Winnie commented.

"Eh, maybe." Abel rolled his eyes in a *not my problem* gesture. "Whatever it is, it means that some people come here and get passed on immediately without hanging around, some—a lot, really—sit tight here until someone among the living is willing to vouch for them and help them pass on, and some people…well, some people are level threes."

Winnie began to feel a little unsettled. "What happens to level threes?"

"That's where we're headed."

Winnie reared back in alarm. "You're taking us to the level threes? Is that safe?"

Abel shrugged. "It's safe. We won't linger there."

Winnie didn't feel particularly reassured, but she followed along nonetheless.

"Go on, Abel," Nina prompted. "Tell us about this Tod character."

Abel's jaw tightened before he said, "The process should be pretty smooth, okay? A level two anchors with another level two. Let's say, as an example, it's a mother and daughter. Mom's here, daughter's there. With me so far?"

The women nodded.

"Mom will spend her time here checking in with her daughter, maybe, like you saw, sending her little comforts here and there. Eventually, the daughter will die. I'll fetch her, and together we'll find her mom. When the two are reunited, the daughter basically testifies for her mother: 'Yes, she was a good and loving parent. Yes, her loss left an unfillable void in the lives of all who knew her.' Blah, blah, blah."

Winnie rolled her eyes. "What if she didn't?" she asked. "What if she was a crummy mom the daughter wasn't that fond of?"

"Well, that's a problem, isn't it?" Abel conceded. "Some essences pass through quickly. A man may linger here a short time if he's anchored to his brother who passes soon and vouches for him fondly. But if his family disliked him, his wife was happy when he died, and all but his youngest child thought he was a jerk, they each may anchor him in turn and then refuse to testify on his behalf."

"You're saying that if one anchor refuses to vouch for you, you get a new anchor? And then you just hope for the best?"

"Yes. Then, if the last person alive who knew you and could have vouched for you dies and refuses…"

"You could be stuck here forever," Nina finished.

"Got it in one," Abel finished bitterly. "It isn't really *forever*, but it may as well be."

Silence fell among the group until Winnie finally worked up the nerve to ask what she was sure was on Nina's mind as well. "Is that what happened to you, Abel? Are you stuck here because no one vouched for you?"

Abel cast her a sidelong glance, his jowls jumping a bit with each step he took. "Would it surprise you, Winnie? To find out I wasn't well-liked?"

Winnie looked away from Abel's gaze, but on the other side of him, Nina spoke up. "Actually, yes. It would surprise me."

An aw-shucks grin flickered at the corner of Abel's mouth. "Thanks. Maybe I'm improving with time."

"So what—" Winnie didn't get to finish her question. From their right, the sound of a piercing wail cut off her words. The two women froze, but Abel continued walking as if nothing out of the ordinary had happened.

"This is our stop," he called back over his shoulder.

Winnie and Nina locked eyes.

"Do you think he's kidding?" Winnie asked her companion.

"I don't think they keep him here for his sense of humor, Win."

With a sigh, Winnie took Nina by the arm, and they followed their guide.

Abel had turned off the main road and was following a path that led to a stone wall Winnie was sure hadn't been there a moment ago. As she and Nina scurried to catch up, Abel veered to the right to follow the wall and, coming to the end, he slipped around and disappeared behind it. Winnie motioned for Nina to stay back as she approached cautiously.

"Abel?" she called out as she came to the end of the mossy wall. She stopped where Abel had disappeared, peeking around the end of the wall. Her eyes widened.

"Winnie!" Nina stage whispered behind her. "What do you see?"

"Another wall!" she whisper-called back, and Nina's silence was response enough for Winnie to know Nina was as confused by the structure they had approached as she herself was. She rounded the end of the wall and found herself in an open-roofed passageway. To her right, the wall she'd reported to Nina spread away from her, thick brush crowding it and concealing it from view of the road; to the left, it was identical except for the addition of the second wall she'd just rounded. She stood listening for sounds of Abel. None came.

In both directions, she realized, the wall curved away from her. Towering several feet over her head where she stood now, its rough stone surface was pitted and crumbling. Moss coated much of what was visible, and turkey tail mushrooms sprouted from the matter between the heavy stones. Sparse tufts of grass dotted the dusty ground. As she gazed down the dirt corridor, she realized that in addition to the curve, one wall—Winnie instinctively thought of it as the inside wall—was lower than the other. She had the strange sensation of having been drawn into an artist's demonstration of perspective. Was it following the slope of a hill?

She had turned back the way she'd come to tell Nina it was safe to follow when a hand on her shoulder made her jump.

"Holy cats!" she shrieked, wheeling around to see Abel's mopey visage. "Don't do that, Abel! You'll give me a coronary, and then you really will be my tour guide."

"Steward," he corrected her lackadaisically. "Are you coming or not?"

Nina appeared at his side, following the commotion. "We're coming," she said. "We just lost you when you went around the corner."

Abel set off to the left without comment, and the girls followed him. Nina and Winnie hung back so that Nina could walk backward for a few steps and take in the corridor they now followed.

"Are we on a slope? It feels like we're going down a hill," she said, turning to face the right direction again.

"I think so. And I think I figured out why the walls are different. It's a spiral, Nina," Winnie reported quietly. "A spiral cut down into the earth."

"What do you think is at the bottom?"

Winnie frowned. "Wild guess? Level three."

Ahead of them, Abel cleared his throat. The girls quickened their pace to rejoin him, walking in silence as they descended the sloping coil.

They walked for some time before Winnie remembered the conversation they'd been having when the wall had appeared.

"Abel," she said, her voice louder than she anticipated in the close air of the dirt-floored corridor. "You never finished your story."

Abel's mouth compressed once more into a chagrined line, but he sighed with resignation and continued. "I told you that when the system is working perfectly, level twos anchor to level twos, and everything turns out fine. But level threes don't anchor to level threes, which means that some level twos invariably anchor to level threes. When the level three dies, the essence that passes over can't vouch for anyone."

Winnie's head spun as she worked to make sense of that.

"Because level threes are bad, right?" Nina pressed.

"Bad doesn't begin to cover it. Lots of level twos are rotten people, but they aren't innately bad. There are a lot of factors that make people act badly, but the core of what they are isn't itself bad; the badness simply overshadows the good.

"But some essences lack goodness. The words you're using—good and bad—make sense only because you connect them with helpful actions and harmful actions, or right-doing and wrongdoing, but those aren't actual things. They're just manifestations of the composition of each essence."

"And some essences are entirely bad?" Winnie asked.

"Yes."

"That's where you're taking us? Down a giant funnel with only one way out that's filled with bad spirits?"

"Basically," Abel responded as if this were perfectly reasonable.

Winnie stopped walking, and the other two, noticing her absence, paused to face her.

"Abel, this sounds like a terrible idea. What's the point of bringing us down here? I want to help you, and I want to find my sister, but I don't see how this is going to help us do either of those things."

Abel backtracked to face Winnie. "I didn't know it was your sister you were looking for."

Winnie kicked herself for giving away more information than she'd intended. But if she was expecting Abel to be forthright, she supposed she owed him some transparency. "It is. She's been missing for a while, and I have reason to believe she's imprisoned here somewhere."

"But you don't know why? Or how she got here?"

"No."

"And you also don't know how to get her out." It wasn't a question, and Winnie simply nodded in agreement.

"Also," Abel went on, "you've never been here, know nothing about how this place works, and have no clue about where anything is or how to get from one part of it to another. Is that a fair assessment of your situation?"

Winnie, feeling chastised, bit her lip. "Yes, I guess that's all true."

"Then I don't think you have much choice but to trust that I'm taking you in the right direction and accept that there's a reason we're going into this pit."

Without waiting for her response, Abel turned and headed back down the path, not looking back to see whether Winnie and Nina were continuing to follow or not. Nina waited for Winnie to catch up, and the two of them continued to plod, side by side, Winnie's mind swirling with Abel's words.

"Go on then, Abel," Nina called ahead to him. "You were telling us what happens when a level two anchors to a level three."

Abel slowed his pace almost imperceptibly, and the women once again fell into stride on either side of him.

"If a level two anchors to a level three, the level three comes here, or to a place like this, when it arrives." He motioned around at the stone corridor that had become increasingly cooler and darker the deeper they'd wound toward its base. "The level two is in a predicament then, as you can imagine. In the best cases, the level two anchors to someone else."

"Like they do if their first anchor refuses to vouch for them?"

"Right." He turned his head to agree with Nina. "But if that was the essence's last chance, they're permanently unanchored..."

"And stuck here," Winnie finished for him.

He nodded, his wiry hair bobbing with the movement.

"There's something I don't understand." Nina's eyes were glued to Abel's profile, and Winnie was thankful for this distraction, which kept her mind off what was waiting for them up ahead. "You said the reason you're here is because your anchor wouldn't vouch for you. But a while ago you said you'd dug yourself into a hole. What hole?"

"I told—" Abel's answer was cut off by another heart-stopping shriek from the depths of the winding coil, and the hairs on Winnie's arms stood on end. That scream had definitely been closer than the last one they'd heard. They were coming to the bottom of the nautilus-shaped structure.

"As I was saying," Abel continued with the tone of a man who had been rudely interrupted by a fellow guest at a dinner party. "I told you before level twos are my charge. Since I had no anchor, I was assigned to stewardship. And it was going fine, initially." He fell silent, apparently thinking about how to continue his story. Winnie wondered if he'd ever been asked to tell it before.

"There was this girl…"

"I knew it!" Nina interjected, startling both of her travelling companions. "I just knew there would be a girl in this story. What was she like, Abel? Was she beautiful?"

Abel scowled at Nina, displeased either by the interruption or by the suggestion that his story could be so easily predicted. Perhaps by both.

"As a matter of fact, yes, she was. Very beautiful. She was a level two. But she was anchored to a level three, and when he came over, she became unanchored.

"In addition to stewarding newcomers, one of my tasks is to find essences that have become permanently unanchored and resettle them in their new roles."

"They can become stewards, you mean?" Nina was clearly keeping up better than Winnie, to whom this hadn't occurred.

"Yes, among other things. You'd be surprised how many jobs there are here. My job is to find the unanchored essence, present them with a garment like this"—he motioned to the hooded poncho hanging open over his shoulders—"and deliver them to Tod for reassignment."

"Tod is your boss, then?"

"Tod is everyone's boss, sooner or later."

Winnie's brow furrowed at this cryptic response, but before she could ask what he meant by that, Abel continued his story.

"When I found this particular soul, she was…displeased by the turn of events. No one wants to become a wraith, but for the most part—"

"A wraith?" Nina interrupted, and if she heard Abel's huff of annoyance, she didn't let on.

"Yes, a wraith. An untethered essence permanently reassigned in this realm. *Anyway,*" he added meaningfully with a pointed look at Nina, "she proposed an alternative. I mentioned before, I believe, that when an essence over-exerts itself comforting an anchor, it's possible for the anchor to pass over and find no essence to vouch for. When that happens, the newcomer is simply assigned an anchor of its own, and its duration begins without the testimonial process ever taking place. But this woman, the one I was supposed to place as a wraith, proposed I find a newcomer with no essence to vouch for and…recommend to the newcomer that it should instead vouch for her."

"Oh, Abel. You didn't," Winnie said.

Abel scowled again. "I've been here a long time. Wraiths have a term of service; in the absence of someone to vouch for us, we essentially work our way into the next level. Eventually, all wraiths can earn their way out of this place, but we don't know how long that will take."

Nina patted his arm consolingly. "We understand, Abel. Everyone wants to be connected to someone, right? I mean, from the sound of it, that's kind of the point of this whole place. And I'm sure she agreed to do something very…kind for you in exchange."

"I suppose," Abel grunted, but Winnie saw that he at least had the grace to blush. "Anyway, I did it, if you must know." He cast an irritated look in Winnie's direction. "Of course, it went fine. The newcomer, being new, had no idea he shouldn't vouch for a stranger, and the woman passed into…well, she passed. The newcomer was assigned an anchor, and everyone was happy with the arrangement."

"Sounds like there's a *but* coming," Nina suggested.

"But," Abel confirmed, "once the whole thing was done, I realized I still had the hood."

"The hood? Oh…" Nina reached out and plucked at the hood lying limp behind Abel's head.

"What could I do with it? I couldn't very well subject some innocent soul to unending service as a wraith simply to cover my crime. And unlike all other essences, wraiths report directly to the boss. When I saw him next, I had no new wraith with me for assignment."

"What did Tod do?"

"See for yourself." He stopped abruptly, dropping to one knee. Winnie had the irrational thought that perhaps he had to retie a shoelace before remembering the haunting image of his furry metatarsals.

Abel had in fact yanked up his right pant leg, revealing a lower leg as hairy as, apparently, the rest of his slender form. Around his ankle, so fine and pale that it was hardly visible, wound a gold chain.

Nina squatted to get a better look. "What is that?"

"It's my manacle," Abel answered sadly. "It's how Tod will keep me here forever."

Nina's mouth made a concerned O. "You mean as long as you have that, you can't earn your way out?"

Abel nodded, pulling his pant leg back down to cover the thin band. "Not unless Tod changes his mind and releases me. But knowing him, that's not likely. I'd have to do something pretty remarkable to earn my way into his good graces. Not that he has any."

"I'm sorry, Abel." It was clear from Nina's tone that she truly was sorry. "Isn't that awful, Winnie? Winnie?" Nina stood and looked around, but to her surprise, Winnie was nowhere to be seen.

Twenty-Three

"Winnie!" Nina shouted again, panic creeping into her voice. "Winnie, where are you?" Abel had regained his feet, and together they rushed forward down the corridor, which now curved away from them at a sharp angle.

Abel placed a restraining hand on Nina's arm, and she spun to look at him. "What—?"

"Listen," he commanded, putting a bony finger to his lips. "Do you hear that?"

Nina stood silently, straining to hear anything beyond the rushing of her own blood and the rapid thumping of her heart. "No, I…"

But she did, she realized. Faintly, Winnie was saying her name.

Nina turned from Abel and walked cautiously forward, one hand trailing along the mossy wall. She hadn't noticed that, in addition to the corridor's curve becoming tighter, the corridor itself was narrower than before. A few steps farther along, she was able to put out both hands and feel the rough stone against her fingertips on each hand. As Nina moved, she became aware of the unmistakable sounds of people: the murmur of voices and movement. But there was something urgent about the sound, like the susurration of bad news and panic spreading through a crowd.

"Nina?"

Winnie's voice was quiet, and Nina mimicked its low tones. "Winnie? I'm here," she said.

Finally, she rounded the end of the great spiral's inside wall and came face to face with level three. The hardpack floor of the pit spread out before her and from it, round and round, rose the stone coils of the long passage down which they'd trekked. In the center of the pit, an anchor pool identical to the one in the village green reflected the faces of forms that surrounded it.

Unlike the essences in the village green, though, the faces of these men and women were contorted with misery. Rather than casually approaching the pool and searching until they found the face they were looking for, these figures seemed pulled there, moaning and whimpering, against their wills. They gnashed their teeth and raked their hair with their fingernails, fighting what seemed to be an unassailable urge to stare into the shallow water. Once there, their eyes bulged with horror, and their mouths contorted into grimaces of agony. One woman seemed to be silently screaming, and when an airy croak escaped her mouth, Nina realized with revulsion that she was no longer capable of screaming, though she clearly couldn't fight the urge to. Another man, his face deep red with effort, reached toward the pool's surface, his fingers knotted into claws. Yet no matter how forcefully he strained, a barrier Nina couldn't see prevented him from touching the water's surface.

Nina stood transfixed, staring in shock at the unspeakable bedlam before her. As one figure fell away, choking and weeping, another took its place, and the whole horrible process began again. The figures milling about the pit babbled incoherently, chattering not to one another but to themselves, twitching and frantic, casting the occasional desperate glance at the pool.

Nina's eyes jumped from one scene of misery to the next, searching with growing panic. Then, Nina's heart stopped. One of the forms transfixed by the pool was Winnie.

"Winnie!" Nina gasped, but before she could make a move, Abel had shot past her and skidded to a stop behind Winnie. Carefully, his eyes unfocused and his head turned away from the pool, he reached up to Winnie's face and covered her eyes.

"Help me, Nina," he called back over his shoulder. Nina rushed to stand beside him, tense and ready to do what he asked. "Take her hand. Pull her away from the pool, gently. And whatever you do, don't look in the pool."

Nina followed his instructions, grasping Winnie's hand and tugging gingerly. At first, Winnie didn't move.

"Come on, Winnie. Come away now," she whispered softly.

"Nina...," Winnie murmured, her voice ragged.

"It's me, Winnie. And Abel. Turn and come with us," Nina coaxed.

Slowly, Winnie began to turn toward Nina's voice. Abel's long fingers crushed her white-blond hair against her temples as he fought to keep her eyes covered while he moved with her turning form. Nina reached out for Winnie's other hand; she began gingerly walking backward, leading Winnie by both hands, as Abel followed awkwardly behind.

"Don't go back the way we came," Abel cautioned Nina. "There's a doorway to the wraith chambers. That's why we came down here. Look over your right shoulder."

Nina glanced in the direction Abel jutted his chin and saw an archway cut in the stone walls of the pit. Within its depths, on the other side of a shadowy vestibule, she could see the dim outline of a door. She turned them toward it.

"This should be far enough," he said when they'd made it through the archway and out of sight of the anchor pool. Nina pulled them into an alcove inside the archway where the noise of the tormented creatures they'd left behind, though muffled, formed an unpleasant soundtrack to their ministrations. Abel removed his hands, but Nina kept a tight hold of her friend, watching Winnie's face anxiously as she blinked like she'd just come from a dim room into bright sunlight.

Abel had come around to Winnie's side. "Back with us?" he asked, and Nina was touched to hear concern in his voice.

Winnie looked into Nina's eyes. Tears pooled on her bottom lashes. She said nothing but leaned forward into Nina, who let go of her hands to wrap her in an embrace.

"Oh, Nina," she whispered tearfully into Nina's hair. "It was awful. I can't tell you how awful it was."

"It's okay now, Winnie. You're safe here with Abel and me."

Winnie sobbed, and Nina stroked her back gently, making formless little shushing noises against Winnie's ear.

After a while, Winnie's sobs slackened, and finally she pulled away from Nina and wiped her eyes with the back of her hand.

"I'm okay now, I think," she said, hiccupping for punctuation.

"What happened back there?" Nina asked, but Winnie could only drop her head, unable to answer.

"I think I can answer that," Abel volunteered. "I owe you an apology, Winnie. I should have warned you before we got to the bottom about what you'd see there."

"I just peeked around the corner," she murmured in a small voice. "I saw the pool, and I couldn't stop myself from looking into it. It was like it was…pulling me."

Nina's forehead creased in concern. She turned to Abel. "What did we just see? What was that, Abel?"

"Level threes have anchors just like level twos. The difference is that unlike level twos who anchor to a person they loved in life, and who hopefully loved them in return, threes anchor to all the people they harmed."

"All of them?" Nina repeated, swallowing a sick feeling.

"All of them. And unlike twos, who share both the good and the bad of their anchors' lives, threes see only the joys."

"But all that screaming and misery…"

"Remember when I said level threes are essences who lack goodness? What you saw back there were souls of pure darkness being exposed to light. Bad being exposed to good."

"Like being burned alive," Winnie muttered.

"But that can't be what Winnie saw, Abel. She's not evil or dark or whatever."

"I didn't see what they were seeing, Nina. I just saw them. Those things back there. I just saw them in the water, screaming and fighting and ripping their own hair out."

"Oh, Winnie," Nina wrapped an arm around her friend and pulled her close.

"I couldn't move. I couldn't stop looking. I couldn't stop feeling what they were feeling."

Nina looked at Abel questioningly.

"That's another difference with the anchor pool here. The spirits can't resist it. They fight to get away from it while it's torturing them, but as soon as it releases them, it wants them to come back."

Nina shivered. She thought of the men and women cowering around the edges of the pit, whom she took to be muttering to themselves. But it wasn't their own voices they listened to; it was the voice in the pool, calling them back again and again. She hesitated to ask her next question, but she simply had to know its answer. "The man—the essence, I mean—reaching for the water?"

"It won't permit itself to be touched," Abel responded. "After all, if an essence connects with an anchor, they disappear for some time. The pool won't allow threes that benefit. They want to disappear, but they can't."

"That's awful. That's so awful," Nina spoke almost to herself.

To her great surprise, it was Winnie, still pale and shaking from her ordeal, who responded. "It's fair, Nina."

Nina turned a surprised look on her friend.

"Those people out there caused nothing but misery and pain in their lives." Winnie's voice shook, but Nina realized it was from anger rather than sorrow. "They did things to people who were weaker than them, and they had no remorse. What's happening to them is fair."

Nina, who was afraid to ask what else Winnie had seen when she'd looked in the pool, said nothing. The three of them stood there silently, each lost in contemplation of the torture they'd just witnessed.

Abel's head suddenly shot up, and he spun to peer around the corner of the archway into the pit.

"Abel?" Nina asked, fear making her voice small. "What's wrong?"

"Listen," he answered. "What do you hear?"

Nina and Winnie attended silently, their eyes wide with concern.

Finally, Winnie answered, "I don't hear anything."

"I don't either." He turned to look at Nina.

When she met his eye, Nina swallowed. In a whisper she asked, "Why have the threes gone quiet?"

Twenty-Four

Winnie felt the crackle of terror that flashed between her two companions. "What's happening? Nina? What's going on? Abel?"

"Someone knows you're here." Abel's face had turned the color of skim milk.

He was backing up into them away from the archway. Nina put her hands up to arrest his movement, and it seemed to remind him of the women's presence. He spun around and stared at them blankly.

"They're coming."

Nina made a sound between a squeak and a moan and clutched her throat.

"Abel," Winnie said, surprised at how steady her voice was after having just wept a wet spot on Nina's shoulder. "Open. That. Door."

Abel gaped at her before scurrying to the doorway. He placed his hands flat against the door, whispered an inaudible phrase under his breath, and pushed.

Nothing happened.

"No," he muttered in disbelief. He cast a glance over his shoulder. The girls were behind him, their faces masks of terror, but he saw them only briefly, for his gaze was drawn immediately to the mass of forms moving with mute concentration toward them on the other side of the archway. "It didn't work."

"Try it again," Winnie commanded. "Just focus and try again."

He took a deep breath and repeated the process, flattening his hands on the wall until his fingernails turned white and spitting the whisper desperately at the unyielding stone before him. He closed his eyes and pressed his shoulder to the door, but again nothing happened.

Nina looked at Winnie, terror contorting her face. "What are we going to do, Winnie?"

Winnie swallowed, overcome by fear. "Abel, is there any other way out?"

"Look around us, Winnie! We're at the bottom of a pit surrounded by solid rock!"

Rock! The word rattled in Winnie's mind. If her father were here, he'd use the rock to his advantage. She couldn't do that, but...

"I have an idea," she said, and she thrust Nina behind her and turned to face the wall of malevolent spirits that was now crushed in a bottleneck at the archway on the other side of the vestibule.

The faces of the mass that pursued them made her gut tighten painfully. Eyes that had been enthralled by the anchor pool glared hatefully at the three of them. The phantoms' movements were slow and deliberate, and Winnie had the bizarre impression that, though there were hundreds of individual forms, they seemed to move in tandem, as though a single powerful force controlled the many moving parts of the level threes.

Pushing aside her fear, she closed her eyes. She pictured the anchor pool, fixing the sight of it in her mind even though its memory made her want to weep again. She held her hands out before her, channeled her magic, and spoke.

"Freeze."

The hair on the backs of Nina's and Abel's necks prickled with the surge of magic, and as they watched, murky water snaked in rivulets around and between the feet and legs of the oncoming spirits, freezing in place as it went. It coiled up the limbs of the front row of creatures and halted their forward progress. The first few essences that had made it through the bottleneck in the archway made to lurch forward but found themselves frozen in place by vines of ice. The pack behind them, moving as they did in uncanny tandem, moved forward anyway, crushing against the front row. Some of the closest spirits bent under the weight of the crushing crowd, and the gunshot cracks of breaking ice pierced the air. Winnie cringed at the thought that more than ice was breaking under the onslaught.

"Winnie, they're still coming. We need more ice!" Nina's voice was urgent in Winnie's ear.

It took all Winnie's concentration to maintain the very specific pattern of ice required to stop the horde, and she struggled to sustain that concentration and respond to Nina. "I can't make more, Nina," she murmured through gritted teeth. "There wasn't that much water in the anchor pool, and there just isn't any other water here."

"The dead don't drink," Abel said, somewhat unhelpfully.

"What are we going to do if we can't find more water?" Panic edged Nina's voice.

Winnie felt that panic, too. The first line of spirits had been crushed under several subsequent lines so that the mass of oncoming fury climbed over a rising, grunting berm of moving creatures. Because she needed water to freeze the still-mobile beings at the top, she drew it up from the bottom of the pile; now, less ice secured the figures at the bottom, and what she could move up wasn't enough to arrest the creatures at the top. All in all, she was losing the battle.

"I don't know what to do, Nina!" She was furious with her limitations, furious that without her mother's help, even her own formidable magic was insufficient. Mostly though, she was furious that she had brought Nina here with her and now wouldn't be able to get her back out.

"I need more water!" She shrieked in desperation, tears forming in her eyes like a mockery of the very liquid she needed. They ran down her cheeks in a stream. A sizable stream. A stream that suddenly seemed much too great to be tears, actually.

Winnie looked up, her concentration breaking so completely that the last of her icy barrier shattered and fell before the powerful surge of creatures behind it. Beings that had been straining against it tumbled forward when the blockade unexpectedly gave way and sprawled pell-mell in the dirt at their feet.

Winnie heard the commotion, but she was focused on the sight above them.

"Thanks, Mom," she whispered, as a spurt of crystal-clear water that had been only a sprinkle at first gained pressure and began to geyser from a crack in the rock above them.

"Freeze it, Winnie!" Nina screamed behind her, and with a pulse of powerful magic, Winnie did just that.

The drenching waters hardened in an instant, stopping the closest spirits in the span of a heartbeat. As the water from above continued to pour down on them, Winnie repeated the freeze command again and again, until the only sound in the space was the rush of water.

Panting with exertion, Winnie looked down at her feet. A lone hand jutted from the mass of ice and bodies, it's index finger inches from her leg. As she watched, it twitched feebly.

She turned to look at Nina and Abel. They, too, stared at the icy hill of bodies.

The rush of water slackened and finally slowed to a trickle. Winnie looked up at the fissure where the water had split the rock and smiled.

"Winnie?" Nina's voice was a hoarse croak.

Winnie looked at her friend, who had pushed her damp bangs to one side and was trying without much success to dry her glasses with the hem of her wet tunic.

Nina put her glasses back on and grinned. "That. Was. Awesome."

Winnie grinned back and threw her arms around her friend, squeezing her tightly with relief.

"I'm sorry to break up this tender moment, but we still have a substantial problem."

Winnie and Nina broke apart and turned to look at Abel. He was studying the door, but he looked at Winnie when he realized he had their attention. "You might have mentioned the magic thing."

Nina bristled visibly. "And you, sir, might have mentioned the 'these things sometimes attack people for no apparent reason' thing."

Abel straightened proudly, which put him only nose-to-nose with Nina.

"Level threes don't attack people for no reason."

"Oh, no?" Nina challenged him. "Then how do you explain what happened out there?"

"Easy. You ladies don't belong here, which wasn't a big deal until your girlfriend decided to do the one thing I told her not to do. She shouldn't have looked into that pool. Now the powers that be are launching a defense."

Winnie studied Abel. "Those spirits were being controlled. That's why they moved the way they did, right? One person was controlling them. That's what you're saying?"

"Exactly. I don't know how you summoned that water, but just because it stopped those things doesn't mean it solved our problem."

Nina harrumphed her disapproval of Abel's thanklessness.

"Look around us, Nina," Abel commanded sternly. "This door won't open. That archway is blocked by a mountain of frozen essences. We're standing ankle deep in water under enough stone to bury us for eternity." He turned to Winnie. "So, unless you can magically move rock like you do water,"—here he wiggled his fingers derisively like a birthday party magician—"we don't have much chance of rescuing ourselves, much less your sister."

He turned his back on the two women to ponder the stone door before them. Nina looked at Winnie, her mouth hanging open in awed realization, and Winnie felt her heart swell. She reached forward and tapped

Abel's shoulder. When he turned back to look at her, she grinned.

"Stand aside, Abel. It's time to move some rock."

Twenty-Five

Winnie thought her words had sounded pretty smooth when she'd ordered Abel aside, but as she stood looking at the door, she realized she didn't actually know how to open it. How *had* she just summoned her mother?

A few moments of anticipatory silence passed as Winnie stood unmoving before the door, but after several minutes had ticked away, Winnie felt Nina move to stand beside her.

"Go ahead, Winnie. We're ready," Nina whispered.

Winnie frowned. "Umm...," she answered unhelpfully.

"I don't mean to pry," Abel chimed in from behind them, "but can we move this along a bit? The ice is starting to melt."

Winnie turned to scowl at him, but she acknowledged the increase in sounds from the frozen hillock behind them, including several ominous cracks.

"How did you get your mom to help?" Nina prodded, and Winnie turned to her and shrugged. She was going to have to admit she didn't know what to do next, even though she could feel Abel's gaze burning through the back of her head.

"You got me. I don't know what to do next. Mom and Dad are clearly up there somewhere, keeping an eye on us. But I don't know how to communicate with them."

"Mom and Dad?" Abel's tone, to Winnie's relief, was curious rather than derisive.

"Winnie's folks are Elementals. Her mom controls water, and her dad controls rocks and stuff."

"Huh. And she makes ice?"

"Winter," Winnie cut in. "I do winter."

"Interesting," Abel observed. "If you don't mind me asking, what does your missing sister do?"

"She—" Winnie's mouth snapped shut, cutting off her answer. The thought of her sister triggered a rush of thoughts and questions, and they flooded her mind in such a jumble that she had to turn away from Abel and Nina to sort through them.

She felt a hand on her shoulder.

"Winnie? Are you okay?" Nina's concerned voice cut through Winnie's swirling thoughts.

"Nina! When we were looking at the maps, neither of my parents could see exactly where Vee was, right? I mean, they could see that she was here, but they couldn't do anything to help her."

"Right...," Nina agreed, but it was clear to Winnie that she wasn't seeing the significance of this.

"And even though we've been down here for...well, I don't know how long we've been down here, but however long it's been, in all that time, they haven't intervened. So, what happened to let them know where I was and what I needed?"

Nina pursed her lips as she thought. "Well, for one thing, they know where to look. They didn't know she was here, so they weren't looking here." Her eyes widened. "But once she did magic, they were able to trace it!" Her expression shifted to one of confusion.

221

"Why aren't they helping her now, then? If they know she's here…"

"She must not be using her powers, Nina!" The delight of figuring out the answer to the question swelled within her and then evaporated in an instant.

Seeing Winnie's look of dawning concern, Nina wrapped a protective arm around her. "Hey," she murmured. "Hey, don't jump to conclusions. There are lots of reasons she may not have used her magic since she sent that message, Winnie."

"Like what? Besides the obvious one, I mean," Abel wondered aloud behind them, earning him a furious scowl from Nina over her shoulder.

"Don't listen to him," Nina urged.

"I always assumed it was a message from her. An SOS. It never occurred to me she was…that it might have been her last…" Winnie couldn't finish the sentence.

Nina grabbed her firmly by the shoulders. "And you still don't know that's what it was. The only way we're going to find out what happened is by doing what we came here to do. We clearly can't go back," she pointed out, casting a nervous glance at the slowly thawing mass behind her. "So we might as well keep moving forward. Come what may."

Winnie nodded determinedly. Nina was right.

"Okay, I think I have to work my own magic here so that Dad knows what I need. Help me, you two." She squatted down and collected palmfuls of the water that still pooled around their ankles; then, she briskly smeared the water on the rock around the jamb of the unopened door.

Working together and moving rapidly to prevent the water from drying before Winnie had the chance to do what she needed to do, the three of them dampened the rock surrounding the door. Then, Nina and Abel stood back, giving Winnie what little space they could so that she could summon her element.

With a hand pressed flat to either side of the door, she summoned her magic and spoke her command. Ice crystals spread outward from her fingertips, traveling speedily across the damp rock until a crystalline garland surrounded the door.

"Help me, Dad," she whispered.

With a familiar rumble, the rock beneath the thin layer of ice began to crack. Winnie stepped back as chips and dust began to shower down, plunking softly in the water at their feet.

"It's working!" Nina trilled in delight, grabbing Winnie with both arms and squeezing her joyfully. "Thanks, Pete, wherever you are!" she crowed with her head thrown back.

All three of them turned their faces away as, with a final, reverberating crunch, the stone door tipped and fell backward, slamming onto the stone floor beyond the doorway and sending up a silty cloud.

Swatting at the air before them and coughing, the three curious travelers peered into the dark recess revealed by the now-missing door.

"Huh," Abel said into the silent space beyond. "Neat."

Winnie turned to him. Rock dust clung to his bushy eyebrows, and his pale face was gray with grit. One glance at Nina told her they all seemed to be in the same condition. Winnie could only imagine what she herself must look like.

"Okay, Abel. I've opened your door. Lead on."

"Me?" he asked, aghast.

"Yes, you. You brought us down here to come through this door, remember?"

He snorted. "Yeah, well a lot's changed since then. None of this is normal. That"—he pointed at the essence iceberg behind them—"is not normal. The door refusing me entry is not normal. You and you"—more pointing—"are not normal. I can only imagine that trend is going to continue once we go through that door."

Nina reached out to stroke Abel's arm tenderly. "It's okay, Abel. We understand."

"You do?" Abel sounded relieved.

"Absolutely. And I want you to know Winnie and I will be right behind you." She smiled sweetly and pushed him through the open doorway.

Winnie snorted. "Atta girl," she said under her breath.

Abel tripped on the lip of the door that now lay like an area rug at their feet, but he caught himself with an awkward jog and stumbled to a stop. He turned to glare at Nina, but it was clear his heart wasn't in it. Winnie was learning that yet another of Nina's most loveable qualities was…well, being loveable. Who could be mad at Nina?

"How's it look, Abel?" she called in after him.

Abel made a show of turning in all directions. "It looks like it always looks." Suddenly his head shot up and to the right, peering into darkness beyond the girls' line of sight. "Oh…oh, no…It can't be!" His hands rose to his face in terror. "Not a three-headed dog!" he shrieked.

Winnie and Nina rushed forward in a panic, falling into what had become a natural position of flanking Abel. Winnie's gaze shot around the dim atrium into which they'd run, searching for the source of Abel's fright.

It took her a moment to realize Abel was watching her, his hooded eyes looking even more shadowed in the weak light cast by intermittent flame torchieres lining a path that led away from them through a stone tunnel.

"Made you look," he deadpanned.

"Abel!" Nina tutted, one hand on her hip. "You…," she trailed off, apparently considering what name to call him before punching him in the arm instead.

"Yow!" He rubbed his arm. "You deserved it! You pushed me through the door."

Nina clucked dismissively and turned away.

"You didn't really think there'd be a three-headed dog, did you?" He'd turned to Winnie, still rubbing his sore arm.

"Cut us some slack, Abel. It's our first time hanging out with dead people."

"And some of them just tried to eat us," Nina added.

Abel scoffed. "You're thinking of zombies."

Nina considered this. "Okay, maybe you're right. Either way, it's been a weird day." She turned to survey the cavernous room they'd entered. "But this looks promising. Where are we?"

"The wraith quarters," Abel said, stepping down off the door and heading for the torch-lined corridor. "This is where I live. Where all the wraiths live, actually."

"Oh, cool," Nina said with genuine enthusiasm. "You're taking us to your place?"

"No." His short response made Nina's face fall. "This is also where wraiths report for assignment."

Nina looked at Winnie quizzically. Winnie stopped, slapping her forehead, stupefied by her own stupidity.

"Winnie? What is it?" Nina backtracked to Winnie's side.

Taking a deep breath, Winnie turned to Abel, who had turned to look at her but wasn't coming any closer.

"Abel, back at the door, you said I shouldn't have looked in the pool. You said the powers that be were launching a defense against us."

Abel stared at her but said nothing.

"I asked you if you meant someone was controlling those spirits, and you said yes. Who was it, Abel?"

Nina turned slowly to face Abel, scrutinizing his face.

"Abel?" she said quietly.

"I'm sorry," he whispered, and Winnie could see from the look on his face that he meant it. "I told you it would take something big to get this thing off my ankle."

Winnie's rage swelled inside her like a tidal wave. "You sneaky little rat! That's why you took us down into the pit! You weren't leading us to find my sister! You were turning us in to your boss!"

Winnie felt Nina tense beside her, but rather than the angry outburst she thought was coming, Nina's voice came out small and hurt. "How could you betray us, Abel? We promised to help you."

Abel's expression seemed to break, and he turned away from them, shame weighing down his shoulders.

The two women watched him disappear down the dim corridor.

"What do we do now, Winnie?"

Winnie bit her lip, anger, betrayal, and fear washing over her in relentless waves.

"I don't know," she whispered.

"I do," said a voice behind them, and both women spun in shock to find themselves looking up into the black eyes of Tod.

Twenty-Six

"Son of a—"

"Tod, I presume?" Winnie cut off Nina, who clutched her chest, gasping to catch the breath that had been startled out of her.

"I don't know who you are, but you shouldn't be here," Tod said curtly.

His tall form towered over Winnie, but Winnie didn't feel cowed. She'd had her fill of feeling overwhelmed and overpowered. She was tired from the day's long walk, or several days, if she thought about it clearly. Time didn't seem to function the right way here.

In fact, nothing was functioning right: she was dirty and bedraggled, her clothes stiff with rock dust that had clung to her damp tunic and dried into a filthy crust. She could feel grit between her toes.

And that was the least of her problems. She felt exhausted by the fight with the level threes, spent from the constant use of her power, fed up with the whole prospect of being where she was and having to do what she was doing.

She was angry that her sisters weren't by her side, resentful that it had to be Nina here facing down this challenge when none of this was Nina's fault or responsibility. She was angry at her mother for picking a fight before she left and at her father for not standing up for himself or for her.

She was even mad at Verna for luring her here to what was almost certainly going to be the end of her life. And she was furious at Abel for being a cruddy little turncoat.

But just at the moment, with her nerves frayed beyond belief and the last of her resilience melting away like the last remnants of the last snowstorm of the year, she was just plain old pissed off at Tod.

"Well, I don't know who *you* are," she snarled, "but you shouldn't be so pale!"

Her word echoed down the corridor, and in the ensuing silence, she felt Nina's puzzled gaze. Tod stared down at her, his arms crossed over his chest. He didn't move, but one black eyebrow rose slowly until it disappeared under his untidy, dark hair.

"Winnie," Nina whispered, though Tod was only inches away and could certainly hear every word. "What are you talking about?"

"I don't know!" Winnie cried, throwing up her hands and spinning away from Tod's black-eyed gaze. "I'm tired and mad and frustrated, Nina! I'm mad at stupid Abel for being a ratfink, and I feel like we've been busting our humps for so long against such long odds just to end up getting murdered in a cave by one of the Addams family."

Nina glanced at Tod nervously. "I'm sure she didn't mean that."

His other eyebrow raised. "Your name is Winnie? Is that short for something?"

Winnie had just been getting herself under control, but at this ridiculous question, her anger flared once again.

"My name doesn't matter!" she spun and shouted at the tall, white form before her. "Do you know what matters, Tod? You tried to kill us!"

"You came into my realm!" Tod's arms uncrossed for the first time and fell to his sides, his hands balled into fists. "You trespassed, you used my anchor pool, you tried to use a wraith door…What did you expect me to do?"

Winnie was too angry to weigh whether that was a fair question or not.

She stomped up to Tod, poking him in the chest with one grimy finger, and opened her mouth to speak.

But before she could, a voice from behind her, a voice she recognized, said, "Winnie?"

Winnie spun, open-mouthed, and gaped incredulously at the healthy, lovely form of Verna.

"Verna?" Her voice came out muffled and weak, and though she willed her feet forward to confirm that what she was seeing was actually real, she found that they refused to obey. Without warning, she fell to her knees.

"Winnie!" Verna and Nina said it simultaneously, but by the time Verna had crossed the stone floor between them, Nina was already kneeling at her friend's side, brushing dirty hair out of her eyes.

Verna kneeled before her sister and reached out to grasp her elbows. "Winnie, are you okay? Where did you even come from? How did you get here?" She didn't pause to give Winnie time to answer.

"Verna, you're okay? We came here to rescue you."

"Oh, Winnie!" Verna wailed, and she wrapped her sister in an embrace. "You got my message!"

"What message?" Tod's baritone drew the attention of all three women. Winnie's head snapped around as if she'd forgotten he was standing behind them.

Verna stood up and met his black eyes. "Remember the thyme?"

"The time when...?" he prompted.

She rolled her eyes. "Not *time*, dummy. *Thyme*. The plant."

He chuckled. "Of course I remember." His eyes widened. "You did that to lure me into your cell. Right?"

Verna smirked. "You wish. I did it to find a way to get a message to Winnie. I guess it took a pretty long time for it to reach the surface."

"Wait, *cell*?" Winnie scrambled to her feet and glared at Tod. "You kept my sister in a cell? Like a prisoner?"

Tod put his hands up defensively. "I can explain."

"You can explain putting my *sister* in a *prison cell*?" Winnie's incredulity sent the pitch of her question so high her voice cracked.

"That was a long time ago. I was desperate."

"Desperate for what, Tod? To have your ass kicked by me when I found out you'd imprisoned my sister?"

"Winnie!" Verna exclaimed, a note of reverence in her voice.

"It's a long story," Tod said soothingly. "If you'll hear Verna and me out, I think we can explain everything."

231

Winnie narrowed her eyes, glaring at Tod skeptically. Then she swung around to face Verna. "Is he serious?"

Verna wrapped her arms around her sister. "He's serious, Win. I'm so glad you're here, but I sent that message a long time ago. A lot has changed since then."

Winnie swallowed, feeling swamped once again by the onslaught of emotion she and Nina had endured.

"Oh!" She pulled away from Verna. "I should have said. This is my friend Nina. I wouldn't be here if it weren't for her."

Verna released her sister and wrapped a surprised but compliant Nina in a hug. "Thank you, Nina. Thank you for bringing my sister to me."

"It was my pleasure. Winnie really did all the work; I just helped," she said as Verna moved to Tod's side. Nina smiled at Winnie, but Winnie could hardly muster the energy to do more than grin wanly.

"As long as you're making introductions, I suppose I should as well," Verna said. "Winnie, Nina, I'd like you to meet Tod." She smiled as she looked up into his pallid face. "My husband."

That was the last thing Winnie heard before she fainted.

Twenty-Seven

Winnie opened her eyes. She was lying in a comfortable bed in a stone-walled chamber. A single candle on the bedside table showed her little of the room's detail, aside from a dresser with a ewer and basin, a wardrobe, and…

"Abel!" Winnie hissed as she sat bolt upright. It was only after she'd done so that she thought to look down and make sure she was fully clothed. She was; someone had slipped her out of her filthy trousers and tunic and into a plain white night dress. Or perhaps no one had, and the same force in this place that had dressed her in the tunic without her knowledge had redressed her for bed. Whoever or whatever had redressed her had also cleaned her up: when she raked her fingers through her hair, it was soft and clean.

She turned her attention back to Abel. "What are you doing skulking around my bed? Isn't there a baby somewhere you should be stealing candy from?"

Even in the meager light from the candle, Winnie could see hurt pass over Abel's features, and for just a moment she felt a stab of guilt.

"Tod asked me to see if you had woken up yet, and if so, if there was anything you needed. Is there?"

"I guess not. Where's my sister?" Asking the question sparked her anger again, but it wasn't the emotional avalanche it had been in the tunnel when they'd come face-to-face with Tod. "Actually, there is something you can do for me, Abel. You can tell me how you managed to keep such a straight face while you lied to Nina and me from the minute we came through that door."

Abel sighed and sat down on the side of the bed. "You're giving me more credit than I deserve, Winnie. I've already told Nina all this."

"Well, now you can tell me."

"I didn't know who you were, or who Verna was...none of it. Do you really think Tod, the powerful, Fundamental ruler of death, confides his plans in me? I'm a level two wraith, Winnie. That's like a king running his ideas by the guy who scrubs his royal chamber pot."

"Chamber pot? Jeez, Abel, how long has it been since you were alive?"

Abel glowered at her, and Winnie sat back against her pillows, motioning him to continue with a wave of her hand.

"Tod summoned me and gave me an assignment. Meet you two and deliver you to him. That's what he told me to do, and that's what I did."

"That's it? That's your whole story?"

"Look at it from my perspective, Winnie: how could I have known Mrs. Tod was the person you were trying to rescue? She's not a prisoner, and she never gave the impression she needed rescuing. Tod felt two living beings enter a portal. He sent me to collect you to see what you were doing where you didn't belong."

"He tried to kill us, Abel!"

"You looked into the anchor pool. He saw you as a threat."

"You're defending him?"

"I'm explaining him," Abel corrected her. "I hope you're willing to listen to explanations."

"Oh?" Winnie asked petulantly. "Why is that?"

"He's your brother-in-law, remember?"

Winnie lay in bed for a while after Abel left, hashing over everything that had happened. Once she had digested Abel's words, she rose and scrubbed her face. When she opened the wardrobe to see if it might contain something she could change into, she discovered a full-length mirror hanging inside the door. She was surprised to discover that she was in fact already completely dressed. She looked down to confirm that she was indeed wearing the tunic and trousers her reflection showed.

"I've got to get out of this place," she muttered to herself, crossing the room and slipping out the door.

The sound of laughter in the hallway surprised her; the fact that she recognized it as Nina's laughter surprised her even more. She followed it, moving in and out of the flickering light of wall sconces as she walked.

The hallway emptied out into a long, low-ceilinged room dominated by a heavy, polished wood table. At least twelve chairs surrounded it, and at the moment, Nina, Verna, and Tod occupied three of them.

Tod, Verna's husband, she reminded herself.

"Winnie!" Verna exclaimed as she entered the room. She jumped up to greet her sister, enfolding Winnie in her long, slender arms. "Do you feel better? I was scared when you fainted. Tod moved so fast; he caught you before you hit the ground." She turned an affectionate look on Tod, who grinned sheepishly and peered down into his cup.

Winnie wondered what she was expected to say to this. "Umm…thanks, Tod."

He waved away her thanks and gestured for her to sit.

Winnie slid into the seat next to Nina and watched silently as a woman wearing a wraith's poncho identical to Abel's set a glass of wine before her. Verna leaned forward from her chair beside Tod and pushed a plate of soft white cheeses, shining olives in several shades of green, red, and black, and fat purple grapes closer to her. Winnie picked a bunch of grapes and placed one in her mouth gingerly.

Silent tension seemed to hold the table hostage. No one spoke. Winnie felt the weight of the quiet and began a countdown to Nina filling the silence in her head.

Three…Two…

Nina turned to her and chirped, "Winnie, Verna and Tod started to tell me a little about what happened and how she got here, but we decided to wait until you were up to go through everything. Just so they wouldn't have to repeat it all."

"Okay," Winnie agreed. Even Nina's earnest voice couldn't break through her tense detachment.

Verna looked uncomfortably from her sister to her husband, both of whom were staring down at their laps. "I'm not really sure where to start…"

Winnie's anger fired up again. "Why don't you start by explaining how you managed to get married but couldn't bother to tell your sisters or your parents that they shouldn't worry themselves sick about you?" she demanded. She took a shameful pleasure from watching her sister's face blanch.

"I…I didn't…," Verna spluttered.

"Or maybe you could explain why you never bothered to pop back home to make spring happen so that every temperate region on the planet wasn't thrust into total chaos?"

Tod cringed at the word, but Winnie wasn't interested in his sensitivities.

Verna sat back in her chair, her face now flushed with embarrassment. "I'm sorry, Winnie."

Tod covered his wife's hand with his own. "No," he said, turning to face Winnie. "I'm the one who's sorry."

Winnie looked at Tod. "You're sorry my sister didn't think to tell us she was here, happily married and not in need of rescue? Or you're sorry that—" In a flash, Winnie remembered their brief conversation before she'd fainted. "You said you kept my sister in a cell!"

A charged silence followed Winnie's outburst. Nina said nothing, but Winnie could feel her shifting uncomfortably beside her. Winnie bit the inside of her cheeks. If Nina could advise her now, Winnie was sure she'd tell her to hear out Verna and Tod, to give them a chance to explain. Winnie scooped up a handful of olives; if she kept her mouth full, she'd be forced to keep it shut.

Like a mind reader, Nina spoke up. "Go on, Tod," she said.

"It's true. I kidnapped Verna from her apartment and held her captive."

Winnie inhaled an olive at hearing this, and Nina thumped her a few times on the back to dislodge it.

"Say that again," Winnie prompted, wheezing around the mouthful of olive she couldn't seem to swallow.

"I did something rash and foolish. I had met Verna by chance in the Above. Up there." He pointed at the ceiling, but Winnie assumed he meant back in the realm of the living.

"You can go there? Anytime you want?" she asked, realizing this was hardly the salient point of the discussion but fascinated to discover that while his plane was off-limits to her, hers was hardly off-limits to him.

"Sure," he responded. "There's this door…"

"No more doors, please," Winnie said, holding up her hand. "Nina and I have had our fill today."

Tod grimaced. "Yeah, about that. I'm sorry, Winnie. If I'd known you were Verna's sister…"

"It's fine. I'm sorry we kind of destroyed it."

"How did you destroy it?" he asked, leaning forward. "I get how you froze the threes, but how did you break through the door?"

Winnie caught her sister's eye. "Dad," she said simply, shrugging.

Tod shot a look at Verna. "Your parents can use their magic here?" Verna shrugged in obvious ignorance.

"I don't think they can, really," Winnie said thoughtfully. "Nina and I talked about this. They only helped when my own magic gave them a pretty clear idea of where we were and what we were doing. But they didn't know Verna was here until we asked them to trace the crocus she sent. And even then, they could only tell us she was here somewhere; they couldn't see where she was exactly. Or if she was safe. Or alive even."

Verna looked uncomfortable again, and Nina reached out to stroke Winnie's arm. Winnie crammed a couple more olives in her mouth and gave Nina a weak, thankful smile.

"So, anyway," Verna went on, "I didn't know when I sent you that message that time doesn't run the same way here as it does at home."

"I knew it!" Nina cried, sitting upright with excitement. "I knew we'd been down here a long time. It's moving faster out there, right? Ohh..." she slumped, concern creasing her brow. "I wonder how long we've been gone? My brother will be worried sick if I don't call him soon."

"How much time has gone by, Tod? Up there, I mean," Winnie added, mimicking his previous gesture toward the ceiling.

"Maybe a week?" he volunteered.

"A *week*?" Winnie was shocked.

"Yes!" Verna perked up. "You see what I mean, right Winnie? When I say I lost track of time, I really mean it. Plus, for a lot of time at the beginning, I was in the cell."

"That's right!" Winnie said with feeling, turning her attention back to Tod. She pointed at him accusingly, losing hold of an olive in the process. Nina caught it deftly as it rolled off the table. "You held my sister prisoner!"

Tod had enough shame to look contrite. "I did. I've apologized to her over and over for it." He looked at his wife.

She put her hand on his cheek. "And I've forgiven him." She leaned in to kiss him, but Winnie interrupted the motion.

"Just clarifying here to make sure I've got this all straight," she said acidly. "You've forgiven him for kidnapping you, bringing you to the Depths, and locking you in a cage. Did I miss anything?"

For the first time, Verna showed a trace of impatience. "Yes, Winnie, you're missing something. You're missing Tod opening the door and giving me the chance to walk out of here. You're missing him explaining why he did something so awful, why he felt so desperate that he was driven to do something foolish."

"Oh? I'm all ears. Why did you do it, Tod?"

Tod returned Winnie's gaze. He opened his mouth once to speak, and then closed it again. Still, he studied Winnie's face. Finally, he spoke. "We didn't choose to be what we are. Any of us. But you and Verna have one another and your sisters. I have no one. *Had* no one." He glanced at Verna, who watched him intently. "It was just me here, all alone, for millennia. I got desperate, and desperate people make terrible choices."

Winnie looked from Tod's face to Verna's, and she felt her anger melt just a bit. She was still mad at Verna, and she couldn't pretend to feel as forgiving toward Tod as her sister clearly felt, but she could admit that some things about her sister's relationship were simply none of her business.

"Well, if you're happy, Verna, I suppose that's what matters." Winnie could hear the doubt in her own voice, but her sister didn't seem to notice.

"Thank you, Winnie," Verna's smile was one of genuine happiness.

Nina looked uncertainly back and forth between the two sisters. "So that's that, then?"

"Yes," Verna said with satisfaction. "I believe it is."

Winnie's mouth dropped open. "No, Verna, it definitely is not!" she asserted. "That addresses your situation with Tod, but it doesn't change the fact that you've been missing for over a year, you left your season unattended back at home, your parents and sisters have been worried sick, and Mom and Dad are probably freaking out right now because Nina and I have been off the grid for days. I'm delighted that you're a happy newlywed, but there are definitely some other loose ends that still need to be tied up."

Verna slumped, her happiness deflated. "Oh, yeah."

"You have to come home, Verna. It's fine if you want to live here, but you have to come back for your

241

season. You have to explain yourself to Mom and Dad."

"But Mom's going to kill me, Winnie! She won't understand how easy it was to lose track of time here. And Dad's going to kill Tod." She paled, and Winnie knew that the idea of Brooke killing anyone was surely hyperbole, but that wasn't necessarily true of Pete. What might her father do to the man who had caused so much discord and fear in their family? The man who had stolen his daughter?

But Winnie was tired of worrying about what might happen or who might be displeased. Her gut had an answer at the ready, and she wasn't going to swallow it back down to spare anyone's feelings. Not anymore.

"You're right, Vee. Mom and Dad are going to be furious, and you're going to have to explain this mess and apologize. Then, you'll have to deal with the consequences of your actions. Both of you." She looked pointedly at Tod.

His mouth formed a thin line, but when he spoke, he directed his words at his wife. "She's right, Verna. We've tried to hide for too long. We have to face this."

Verna gnawed her lip, but Winnie could see her resolve breaking.

"But, Tod..." Verna reached out to grasp her husband's hand. He took it, turning to look into her face.

"Go, Verna. I was selfish to bring you here, and I'd be selfish to keep you when you are so clearly needed somewhere else. You have a life away from me. My job is to stay here." Tod's voice broke before he could finish speaking.

Despite her resolve not to forgive Tod as easily as her sister had, Winnie felt a twinge of sympathy for the Fundamental. It clearly cost him to send his wife away.

Nina had been listening attentively to this conversation, but she leaned toward the couple to interrupt. "What exactly is your job description, Tod?"

Tod and Verna stared at her blankly, but Winnie only leaned back in her chair and sighed, watching Nina work her magic with a knowing grin.

Twenty-Eight

When Abel entered the dining room to answer a summons from his boss sometime later, he discovered Tod wearing an expression unlike any he'd ever seen before.

"Abel!" Tod hailed him enthusiastically, and Abel pulled up short, cowering a bit at the unexpected greeting.

"Sir?" he responded nervously.

"Come in, Abel. We need to have a meeting, and then I'll need you to pack me a bag."

"A bag, sir?" Abel felt like the ground had shifted somewhat beneath him, and he struggled to get his bearings.

"Yes. Verna and I are going away."

"Away, sir?"

Tod chuckled. "Is that an echo?"

"Echo, sir?"

Winnie rolled her eyes. "They're coming back with me for a while, Abel. I need to get home, and Verna has a job she needs to get back to."

Abel's mouth worked silently for a few seconds as he soaked in this information.

"But...if you...I mean, who...?"

Nina sidled up to Abel. "Hi there, Senior Assistant to the Interim Lord of the Afterlife." Abel gaped at her.

"'Interim Transitional Coordinator' was the name we decided on, I think," Winnie suggested.

Nina leaned in to Abel, shielding her mouth with the back of her hand theatrically and stage whispering, "I personally preferred 'Interim Master of Death,' but I got voted down."

Abel's mouth continued to hang open. "I don't get it," he said finally.

Tod, who had been darting from room to room, gathering belongings and setting things in order ahead of his unprecedented departure, stopped to fill in some blanks.

"Abel, you're being promoted." Abel's mouth snapped shut audibly. "I'm going to be gone for a while, and Nina has agreed to stay here in my place. She's going to be relying on you to help her get comfortable and to answer any questions she might have about how to run this place. Think you can handle it?"

Abel's hangdog features twitched nervously, but his voice was steady when he responded. "Yes, sir. Certainly. But..." Sensing he was treading ground he had no right to tread, he stopped talking abruptly.

"Go ahead, Abel." Tod's voice was uncharacteristically forgiving.

Abel swallowed. "Sir, excuse my impertinence, but why are you leaving?"

Tod studied Abel's face, deciding how to answer. "I didn't pick this job, Abel. And I've been profoundly unhappy doing it for a long time. I thought to bring Verna here to replace me, but that didn't turn out the way I thought it would. Now I have Verna here with me, but keeping her here means keeping her away from her own duties, and that's something we have to deal with.

"So, Nina has agreed to come work for me, standing in here while I'm out there. Think of it as a...restructuring. Verna and I will be focusing on the...growth branch while Ms. Ramirez performs interim duties here in support of our existing brand."

Abel blinked.

"It means Tod's going topside to help Verna, and I'm no longer unemployed," Nina translated happily.

"I see," Abel responded, though it was clear he was bewildered by the turn of events.

Tod rested an unexpectedly brotherly hand on Abel's shoulder, and Abel twisted his head awkwardly to one side to peer at it.

"You can't imagine what it's been like for me, Abel, being trapped here against my will with no end in sight."

Abel's head shot up to stare at his boss, and his mouth twisted sourly. "Yes, sir," he said woodenly.

Nina tapped Tod on the shoulder and raised herself up on tiptoe to whisper in his ear. Tod's eyes widened in comprehension. He turned to Abel.

"I owe you an apology, Abel. Nina reminded me that I manacled you long ago. With your promotion, perhaps it's time some of your old constraints were lifted."

Tod took hold of Abel's shoulder again and murmured, "Release."

Abel's eyes widened, and he dropped to one knee, yanking up his pant leg and running his hands up and down his now un-manacled leg.

He jumped up, grabbing Tod's hand and shaking it exuberantly. "Thank you, sir! Thank you very much!"

Tod withdrew his hand with a slightly nervous smile. At the sound of Verna's voice behind him, he turned with relief. "Ready, ladies?"

Winnie followed her sister into the room, carrying a bag in each hand and marveling at how much her sister had managed to accumulate in a place full of dead people.

"We're all set." Winnie turned to Nina. "Are you sure you've got everything you need?"

"Positive."

"And Tod's shown you the master pool and how to use it?" Verna asked.

"Yep. If I need anything, I know how to get hold of you. Just make sure you keep a dish of standing water out for me."

"Will do." Winnie set down the bags she'd been holding and wrapped her arms around Nina. "Thank you, Nina. Thank you for everything. I couldn't have done any of this without you."

"Oh, Winnie!" Nina squeezed her tightly. She turned her face to whisper in Winnie's ear, "Don't let your mom be too hard on Verna. I don't know for sure, but I bet the reason she came back when you really needed her was because you've shown her what you're made of. She won't underestimate you again."

Winnie drew back, blinking away tears of gratitude. "I'll come back to visit you. Every chance I get," she said, though she had no clue if this was a promise she'd actually be able to keep.

Nina giggled. "Deal," she said. "Bring wine."

Nina and Abel stood side-by-side on a jutting outcrop of rock, watching as the three figures disappeared through the doorway suspended in midair. They waved enthusiastically, and Winnie's returning wave was the last thing they saw as the forms disappeared into the oppressive darkness beyond the doorframe.

When they were gone, Nina turned to Abel. "Now, about that three-headed dog idea you had...what's the policy here on pets?"

Together, the two of them descended the rocky hill, the landscape spreading out uninterrupted around them.

Epilogue

In the noisy heart of a noisy city, a door opened onto a cramped, overstuffed apartment. A slender man, his black hair slicked thinly over a speckled head and his pale lips contorted by a sneer, picked his way carefully through the stacks of paper and piles of debris that littered the room. The feeling of unease that always accompanied visits to his boss's home prickled up his spine.

He knocked on the last door at the end of the perilously littered hallway.

"What?" came a bark from inside the room.

Taking a deep breath to gather himself, he opened the door.

"Sir," he simpered. "There's been a development."

"What kind of development?" demanded the figure seated at a desk scattered with piles of papers and empty cans. The seated man was lit from behind by a row of screens, each broadcasting news stations covering world disasters both natural and manmade. Their mute pictures flashed and flickered, backlighting the figure so that the face turned to the door was cast in shadow. The slender man moved back a step, staying as far from the broad-shouldered man behind the desk as possible without leaving the room altogether.

"The woman…"

"That filthy Elemental, you mean."

"Indeed, sir. She's returned. With Tod."

"Returned to her family?"

"Yes, sir. And Tod seems to be…"

"Seems to be what?" The figure behind the desk's voice dropped dangerously low.

"Staying with her."

This was met with silence, and the slender man closed his eyes, wishing futilely that he didn't have to utter the next sentence.

"And..." A shift in the figure's outline told the slender man that his boss had leaned forward minutely, though his features remained obscured.

"And she's pregnant."

In the shadows, unseen by the slender lackey who skulked away, thankful for having delivered his message and kept his head, Damion Strife smiled. When he leaned back in his chair, patchy light from the screens behind him illuminated a jagged scar running from one high cheekbone to the far corner of a cruel mouth.

"Well, what do you know?" he murmured into the darkness. "Looks like I'm gonna be a grandpa."

Acknowledgements

Thank you...

To George, for reading this book first and for being genuinely excited about every new chapter.

To JAKE, for enduring the process without complaint.

To Al, for predicting this book twenty years ago and still being my friend when it finally came to be. And for being Meri in the real world.

To Alice, for risking an early read.

To Kathleen Jowaski, for being extraordinarily good at editing.

And to Dad, for frequently saying "When are you going to write that book?" to remind me that you always knew I could.

www.ingramcontent.com/pod-product-compliance
Lightning Source LLC
Chambersburg PA
CBHW022158170626
46807CB00005B/2252